Tales Told
Before Cockcrow

fairytales for adults

for Ma & Pa
with de love

Cherry Potts

Cherry
X

Published 2008 by Onlywomen Press Limited, London, UK

ISBN 978-0-906500-95-8

British Library Cataloguing-in-Publication Data
A catalogue record for this book is available from the British Library

Cover design © Spark Design, 2008

Typeset by FiSH Books, Enfield, Middlesex, UK
Printed in Great Britain by Mackays

The right of Cherry Potts to be identified as the author of this work has
been asserted by her in accordance with the Copyright, Designs and
Patents Act 1988

This book is for
Athena Diamantidi Nanda,
Alix Adams
and
Ghillian Potts

Thank you

Alix Adams for her input into Gershwin-singing sirens, and for wanting stories in the middle of the night.

Dusty, Edie, Hattie, Madge and Zappa for exemplary she-lording.

Greg Nanda for the fastidious knight.

Contents

Tales Told Before Cockcrow

Amelia couldn't sleep. She lay in petulant discontent, eyes fiercely open, just daring sleep to lull her into unconsciousness. Sleep, naturally, had more sense than to tangle with her.

'Count sheep, darling,' her old nurse, Sibyl advised, trying for a reasonable tone despite her intense irritation.

'That makes me hungry.'

'Don't be perverse. You are only awake because you ate too much in the first place.'

'Tell me a story, Nana,' Amelia whined, doing her best to sound as though she thought Sibyl's stories quite the best in the world, which, coincidentally, she did. Flattery always worked on Sibyl, and anyway, she hadn't anything better to do. The other option would be to join the gathering of younger adults, who had no interest in the tales of an ancient nanny. Amelia appreciated her where the others, with their thin veneer of uncertain sophistication, despised.

'Very well,' Sibyl said contentedly, settling beside her charge, 'but you must promise not to interrupt.'

The sun sank slowly below the whale humped cliffs. The bullfrogs joined the cicada's continuo. As the shadows merged into dusk, a lone figure on the cliff top turned in valediction to the red stained sea. Below her on the wave caressed strand the others of her kind waited in silent anticipation. Her liquidly beautiful voice rose into the waiting air...

Summer time and the living is easy...

The taverna across the bay was already crowded with

1

its customary population of fisherfolk and sailors – and their doxies. Toothless old men reminisced in corners about their misspent youth or eavesdropped on the conversation of travellers and visiting merchants. The sharpness of charcoal fires mingled with the richness of roasting meat and the sourness of sweat to create a scent unsurpassed in its rankness. One ancient tottered outside to empty his overcharged bladder into the dock, and while so doing, heard the distant strains of the sirens' song...

'Wait a minute,' Amelia said, 'What are sirens doing singing Gershwin?'

'I didn't say I was talking ancient history did I?'

'There aren't any Sirens left.'

'How would you know, Miss Clever?'

'There are no sirens left.' Amelia said with careful emphasis.

'All right then, these sirens have the gift of prophecy, just like me. Satisfied?'

'And they wasted it on Gershwin?'

'I happen to like Gershwin. Anyway songs are important to sirens.'

'Were important.'

'I thought you weren't going to interrupt. Where was I?'

...heard the distant strains of the Sirens' song...

All through the night, I dream of you darling...

'That's not Gershwin, that's Cole Porter.'

'Don't quibble, and don't interrupt,' Sibyl said stiffly, determined that she would get the child to sleep, by hook or by crook. There were ways...

Scarcely pausing to cover himself, the old man staggered back to his cronies,

'Those females are at it again, singing their disrespectful heathen tunes to lure our honest sailor lads to their deaths...all untimely.'

This set the assembled company to tales of derring-do, lost friends seduced to their doom by the harlots over the water. As more retsina was sunk and they topped each other's boasts of personal bravery, they found themselves committed to a foray to catch a siren the very next day. Nobody could quite remember whose idea it had been.

And so, the next day, before the sun had broken through the grape grey clouds, a small group of shivering sailors gathered on the dock, ready to go hunting sirens. The group was smaller than might be expected by anyone who had listened to the retsina talking the night before, but not so small as to allow the jaunt to be called off. And so they clambered into their ships and hoisted their gull-winged sails. The wind swelled, and before they had their anchors properly on board, the breeze was carrying them out into the bay, towards the treacherous teeth of the rocks that hid beneath the wine dark seas.

On the island the sirens stretched to greet the rosy fingered dawn, and sang softly to one another.

One of these mornings, you're gonna rise up singing...

'I knew they'd sing that.'

'Shhh.'

The sirens spread their wings, and leapt into the air, swooping in the thermals above those treacherous rocks, skimming the wave tips with the very edges of their feathers.

'Feathers? I thought they had fish tails.'

'Depends who's telling the story. My sirens have human faces and bird bodies.'

'Except for their titties.'

'Their what?'

'I've seen the pictures. Breasts, all pointy and silly,

sticking out from the feathers.'

'Who's been showing you such unsuitable pictures?'

'Roland.'

'Well, I suppose that was obvious. I can't think why your mother allows him access to that sort of thing. Are you going to listen to this story?'

'Yes, but I've got another question.'

'Yes?'

'Sirens lay eggs?'

'Of course, they're birds.'

'So they wouldn't suckle their young, would they? I mean, they're not mammals.'

'Exactly. I know what you are going to ask. So that the sailors would think they were human, all right.'

'But what about the feathers?'

'From a distance they'd just look like clothes I expect. And it would hardly matter once they'd got to the island.'

'Is that why the feathers are blue?'

'Blue?'

'In the pictures.'

Sibyl shrugged. Roland would have to be spoken to. Amelia really wasn't of an age for that sort of education. She still tended to believe what she was told, unless she knew it was a story. Sibyl eyed Amelia thoughtfully, and decided to abandon sirens for the moment. She launched into a new story, speaking as rapidly as she could to forestall Amelia's protest. Choosing a hypnotic tone of voice, she swayed her head very slightly from side to side as she spoke.

Sleep, you little bugger, she thought affectionately.

Once there was a knight, who had only recently won his spurs, and was really rather inexperienced. He wandered about the kingdom a lot, looking for Damosels to rescue. So one day, inevitably, he found one. This particular Damosel was sitting, minding her own business in her own garden surrounded by flowers, and little animals and all the usual paraphernalia of damoseldom. She was dressed in white Samite, and her golden hair spread over her shoulders like a cloak.

The knight, who was called Gavin, could see all this, because he had scaled the extremely high wall hoping for an apple tree to scrump, as he was hungry. He now sat rather uncomfortably astride the wall, hissing at his horse, which had wandered away from him, and trying not to attract the attention of the enormous wolfhound that was wandering towards him from the garden side of the wall. Not that he succeeded: he fell off the wall with a loud clatter of armour, and concussed himself. Fortunately the hound was quite an amiable beast and did no more than sniff at him. The damosel leapt up scattering flowers and small animals, and had his helmet off in a trice, which as anyone with half a thought in their head would have known was a dangerous thing to do. Gavin blinked blearily at the vision of loveliness leaning over him, and gasped out a protestation of love before he had thought. This set the damosel into helpless giggles, which brought out her father to see what caused such an inane noise to disturb his studies. Now, the damosel's papa was what most people would describe as an ogre, although one who had put aside ogrish ways. In all, a thorough going wimp.

Poor Gavin, seeing this monstrosity bearing down upon his beloved, leaped to his feet, where he wobbled helplessly for a moment, then drew his sword and without the slightest warning nor, one might add, provocation, ran the ogre through the heart. At the sight of her beloved father cruelly murdered, the damosel shrieked, and fainted away. Considerable cacophony ensued, with the wolfhound howling, and all the animals trying to rouse their mistress. Gavin pulled himself together, and finding himself quite unable to awaken the fair damosel, slung her over his shoulder and carried her off, still unconscious, to his horse.

Sibyl looked at Amelia, now fast asleep, and sighed. She was almost sorry not to finish the story, which was one of her favourites, which she had learnt from her nanny, shortly after the event took place. She particularly liked the bit where the damosel grew her second set of teeth and ate Gavin. Silly boy, fancy not realising that the daughter of an ogre would be an ogress.

Sibyl stood and stretched slowly, limb by limb, claw by claw, until her scales rattled softly like a spring shower on leaves. She turned carefully about in the cramped space of the nursery, and slithered out to the library to eye over her treasure, absent-mindedly checking that the book with the obscene picture of sirens was on a higher shelf. Time enough for Amelia to read that sort of thing when her wings were strong enough to carry her up to them.

Sibyl stretched her wings out to their fullest span, and folded them once more with a leathery snap, and stomped away to the cave mouth where Roland and the other youngsters crouched. Sibyl glanced down the valley in a casual show of unconcern, noting that the small line of torches was closer than it had been before.

'She's asleep,' she said at last. Roland turned his yellow gig-lamp eyes on her and grinned, showing splendid teeth and a lolling forked tongue the colour of midnight. The tongue flickered nervously.

'How long for?'

'A year, perhaps two. I haven't tried that spell for a long time, and she is the liveliest little lizard-features I've had to deal with for a very long time. I've left her plenty of food, and instructions, just in case. You and Samantha can close the tunnel.'

Roland rose, and his bulk quite dwarfed Sibyl. Samantha joined him and their heavily muscled forelegs began scratching at the sides of the cave mouth, until of a sudden a soft roar of rock-fall closed in their greatest treasure, their only darling, their hearts' delight. Roland heaved an unhappy sigh, anxious for his beloved younger sister, and then shook himself briskly, setting off a silvery chiming in his scales. What more could he do?

'Right,' he said, glancing wistfully at the dust settling on the newly fallen rock, 'time we were a-moving.'

With no more ado, he unfolded his great sky-blotting wings and thrust with his hind legs, sending his vast shimmering glory out into the thermals. Slowly each of his kindred rose and stretched their wings and thrust off into the starry darkness, sailing down the wind, until the sky was alive with the slow beating of fourteen leathern wings. Only Sibyl remained, too old to fly far, too proud to run away and leave her last treasure, Amelia, whose wings were too young to carry her yet.

When their enemy arrived, he must find one dragon, since failure would send him seeking after the others, hunting them down until he exterminated them all. There had been no need to draw lots. Sibyl had volunteered. There was a convenient cache of jewels easily to hand, Sibyl hoped their enemy would be satisfied and seek no further after the true treasure, hidden safely beyond the fall of rocks.

Sibyl settled down before the blocked entrance to her cave, and watched the slow armada of dragons drift away up the valley, in search of safety, their passing visible only in the sudden vanishing and abrupt reappearance of stars.

Sibyl curled about and rested her nose resignedly upon the tip of her tail. Everything was ready, but still she stirred anxiously. She took a slow, steadying breath, and checked her fire breathing equipment for the last time. All she needed to do now was to wait for the knight to come.

The She-lord and her Tailor

Once upon a time, a long way off, but not as far as all that, there was a queendom ruled by cats. These cats were particularly large, magnificent, and beautiful. They did not know they were beautiful because no one had told them, and being modest, each thought she was the only ordinary moggie in the world; they hadn't invented mirrors.

These cats were matriarchal and although it was technically a queendom, and although they felt they ought to have a queen, the actual qualifications for queenship were lost in the mists of time; they didn't have history either.

What they did in practice was to take turns at being in charge, which was unusual because most cats really like bossing other cats about, and wouldn't normally give up the game once they had the power. Everyone had a go, for six months at a time, which got very confusing, but no one minded much. They all knew they'd get their turn to organise things better, sooner or later. The position of power was known as She-lord.

One day, not long after a new She-lord had been invested, about three weeks actually, a very strange thing happened. A man appeared in the market place. A human man.

This was very unusual, because no humans came to the queendom in the normal run of things. Any trading was done via the donkey clan who made a nice fat profit out of both sides. In fact there was no record of a human coming there before. As previously

9

mentioned, the cats didn't bother with history; they were too busy enjoying themselves.

Anyway, there was much exclamation in the market place and it was decided that someone had better go and get the She-lord, so that she could see this spectacle. After some discussion it was decided which someone would run the errand, and eventually the She-lord made it down to the market place to check out the fuss. She wore the ceremonial robes; the reason for these was also lost in the mists of time. Every one thought she looked very grand. Everyone, that is, except the man.

He, when he saw the She-lord, let out a great gale of laughter. Consternation reigned. There is nothing a cat likes less than being laughed at, except maybe being wet.

The reason the man was laughing was that the ceremonial robes were very tatty.

The robes were tatty because they had been around a very long time. They were also very dirty, with all sorts of stains about the hem and down the front. It was considered bad luck to wash the ceremonial robes – which it would have been; they would undoubtedly have fallen apart at the seams if they had been cleaned.

Also, the new She-lord was especially large, positively statuesque and the robes simply did not fit.

Well: the She-lord was very annoyed at being laughed at, and sat down and pretended to wash her tail to hide her confusion. When she had done, she sat primly and looked down her whiskers at the man. Then she asked him what the purpose of his visit might be.

At this the man bowed very low and said that he was a humble tailor come in search of work in their fine and prosperous kingdom. The She-lord decided to let this little slip pass. Then he came a little nearer and whispered that of course he would not consider offering his services to anyone but the She-lord herself; which was just as well, since no one else wore clothes. Cats can't stand over familiarity, but they do like to be flattered, so the She-lord smiled to herself and twitched her ears, and invited the man back to the palace where she could have a good rummage through his pack.

Back at the palace, the man was treated with courtesy and given a red silk cushion to sit on, which he kept sliding off, as he had no claws to hold on with. He was offered a bowl of cream, which he declined, and immediately spread before the She-lord his wares.

Now the Tailor made a mistake. He looked at the tatters of the robes, and showed the She-lord only his cheap cloth, thinking she would not appreciate its lack of quality. He had forgotten that he was sitting on silk.

The She-lord was not at all pleased at being taken for a fool, and if the man had understood cats he would have got up and started running. The She-lord suppressed the twitching of her tail, and attempted a purr. She decided to play along, giving the tailor enough string to tangle himself in. The She-lord picked out the most garish designs she could find, placing them next to her pearl perfect, creamy fur.

Sighing, she declared that she simply could not decide. At this, the tailor drew from his pack a small mirror, which he held up for the She-lord to get an idea of the effect of a particularly nasty green chintz, which was draped across her shoulders. When she caught sight of herself the She-lord gasped in astonishment.

'Why', she said to herself, 'My fur is far superior to any of this trash.'

She looked anew at the ceremonial robes she had discarded earlier. Then she looked at the furless skin of the tailor and a great rage shook her. She shrugged off the green chintz and purred soothingly at the tailor, who, not being used to the wiles of cats, overlooked the quiver in her whiskers and the twitch in her tail.

Very gently, she rubbed against the tailor, and said 'How very wise of you, O tailor, to have noticed that my robes were unworthy of me. I shall have all your cloth, and have it made into cushions for the kittens, who after all are not respectful of quality.'

The tailor was taken aback by this and asked what she would do about the ceremonial robes.

'I'll have them burnt,' said the She-lord, 'and I'll have a collar made of leather and let my own beautiful fur clothe me.'

'I'm afraid I don't have any leather,' replied the tailor, beginning to be a little worried.

'Don't you?' said the She-lord, 'don't worry. I'll think of something.'

The She-lord smiled into her whiskers.

'You'd be surprised at the resourcefulness of Cats,' she said, and then she opened her mouth very wide, as wide as it would go, so that the light caught on her needle sharp teeth and the pearly pink perfection of her tongue; and then the She-lord bit off the tailor's head.

The Knight Who Didn't

Sir Harold de Mulberry was a new-made knight. He had done all the things necessary to reach this state. In his case this meant that three days ago he was sent off to the King with a letter from his Mother.

Harold spent three hours waiting for the King to see him, and when he was finally announced, it was obvious the King was not pleased to see him. The King was playing dominoes, with his chief advisor and his three wolfhounds.

'Well, Boy,' said the King, taking his eyes off the game long enough to give him a once over.

There stood Harold de Mulberry, in his shiny-bright armour and his deep red cloak, and his sparkly spurs with a crimson-plumed helmet tucked under his arm. One of the wolfhounds whined.

'Well, Boy,' said the King again, 'It seems your Mother wants me to make you a knight.'

'Yes sir,' said Harold, thinking perhaps his armour should have been less shiny, as both the King and the Chief Advisor winced when they looked at him.

The King nodded thoughtfully.

'Well, it had better be done,' he said, 'Knowing your Mother…'

'It won't do,' muttered the Chief Advisor, and the hound that had whined buried his nose between his paws.

'What's that?' The King asked

'What have you done?' The Chief Advisor asked Harold.

Harold looked puzzled.

The problem was, Harold had never *done* anything.

On the journey to the King's castle Harold had met some serfs. 'Oh! Sir Knight, Sir Knight!' They yelled, running to keep up with the steady trit-trot of Harold's smart white destrier.

'I'm not a knight yet,' Harold explained, without slowing down.

'Oh,' the serfs said, momentarily bamboozled. The one with more puff in him kept running.

'Sir!' He shouted, 'Our village is being terrorised by a dreadful Ogre.'

Harold slowed the horse down, but didn't stop. A bend in the road allowed the serf to catch his breath, while Harold rode round him.

'He says he's going to tear us limb from limb and eat *everyone*!' Gasped the serf.

That decided Harold.

'I'm very sorry,' he said, 'but I don't do Ogres.'

The destrier rolled his eyes backwards at Harold and set his ears low in disapproval, but kept on trit-trotting despite the fact that destrier's really ought to galumph, unless they are doing stately pacing.

The serf limped back to the village and sat down with a thump in the middle of the street and wept. When he could, he looked up at the expectant faces about him.

'It's no good,' he said, 'we're doomed.'

'Why?' asked his wife. The serf gritted his teeth, and finally he spat out:

'That was not a knight.'

'Oh,' said his wife. 'That explains it.'

Meanwhile, Harold carried on along the road, hurrying a little to make up for lost time.

At the next village, Harold found the way blocked by a crowd. His heart sank.

'Good Sir Knight!' cried a worthy old gent in a gold chain and fancy waistcoat.

'I'm sorry, Sir,' said Harold, 'but I am not a knight.'

'Oh.' Said the worthy, 'Well I'm sorry to bother you, but you might be able to help.'

Harold put on his polite listening face and resigned himself to some whining.

'For weeks now,' said the worthy, 'a Dragon has been carrying off maidens from our village, and devouring them.' The worthy gave a nod in the direction of the village green, which was not very green any more, owing to dragon-scorching, and at a sturdy post in the middle of the green where a pretty young thing was tethered.

Harold smiled at the pretty young thing, and the pretty young thing smiled back hopefully.

'I'm sure, if you didn't leave young ladies out for him to find, it wouldn't happen,' said Harold.

The destrier curled his lip and snorted, but Harold didn't notice.

'If we don't do that,' said the worthy, 'The Dragon will come and burn the village and us with it.'

'Oh,' said Harold, 'So this is insurance? Well you seem to have it all worked out, so I'll be on my way.'

'So you can't help us?' asked the worthy, hanging on to 'polite' like grim death.

'I'm afraid not, ' said Harold, 'I don't do Dragons.'

There was an angry muttering from the crowd, but the worthy held up a placatory hand and the crowd shuffled away leaving the road free.

So Harold had continued on his way, and here he was at the castle, being asked what he had done. He put his modest face on.

'Oh, nothing, really,' he said.

'Which road did you come by?' asked the Chief Advisor.

Harold gestured vaguely and the Chief Advisor got up from his dominoes, stepped over a hound and peered out of the window.

There was a lot of smoke on the horizon.

'That Dragon's at it again,' he said.

The King shook his head sadly.

'Dragons,' he said, 'What can you do?'

Harold nodded in sorrowful agreement.

'Right-ho,' said the King, 'let's be at it.'

He looked round for his sword, which was nowhere to be seen. He held out his hand to Harold, who, after a moment's confusion, handed his sword over with pride. It was a beautiful sword, and brand-new too.

The Chief Advisor turned away from the window, and inspected the shiny-bright blade.

'That won't do,' he said firmly. The Chief Advisor pulled his own sword from his belt, and handed Harold's sword back to him.

Harold looked at the Chief Advisor's sword all battered and nicked and *very probably sharp*, he thought nervously, as the point whisked past his ear.

The King tapped Harold on each shoulder.

'Protect the weak,' he said frowning a bit, 'Umm, do no wrong... oh yes... and be whatever you have it in you to be.'

Another wolfhound made a soft moaning noise, and laid its head down.

'Right then,' said the King, 'That's you a knight, my Boy. Best regards to your Mother.'

Sir Harold sorted out his sword and bowed, then he wandered off, his brand new spurs chinking as he walked.

The Chief Advisor shook his head.

'He won't do.'

The King gave the Chief Advisor a long, slightly hostile look.

'It doesn't do to know better than the King,' he said coldly.

'I know that,' said the Chief Advisor. 'But I can still beat you at dominoes.'

And they went back to their game.

Sir Harold mounted his destrier and set off on his journey home.

As he rode over the brow of the first hill, he saw a great billow of smoke, and he quickened the trit-trot to a thundering galumph. The destrier enjoyed the stretching of his legs and the crash as he put his armoured hooves to the ground, and he put his ears forward, and his tail up in excitement; this was so much more fun than trit-trotting about keeping clean and tidy.

When they reached the village it was in ruins. There didn't seem to be anyone about, but eventually Sir Harold found the old worthy, his waistcoat badly singed, and his face and beard streaked with soot and tears, sobbing by the well.

'What happened here?' asked Sir Harold in his best reliable-man-in-a-crisis voice.

'The Dragon happened,' sobbed the worthy.

'Which way did it go? Asked Sir Harold.

The worthy pointed, without raising his head.

'Right-ho,' said Sir Harold, and off he galumphed.

At the next village, there were a lot of bodies, but none of them were charred, so it didn't look like the Dragon had been through. Sir Harold picked his way through the body parts until he found someone still in one piece and with a pulse.

'What happened here?' he asked, in his best concerned-at-scene-of-disaster voice.

'The Ogre happened,' said the serf, who was

bleeding rather badly and didn't expect to live.

'Not that you care,' he said angrily, 'You don't do Ogres, do you?'

'Ah,' said Sir Harold, 'But I am a knight now.'

'You'll never be a knight,' said the serf weakly, ' you won't do at all.'

Sir Harold was about to get indignant, but the serf died, so that was that.

As Sir Harold rode up to his Mother's castle there was a big ugly man with a lot of teeth standing outside. Actually he was a *very* big man, with *really lots and lots* of *very* sharp teeth. The Destrier started sidling nervously, this didn't look like his idea of fun at all.

A shadow flitted overhead and Sir Harold looked up.

There was a Dragon overhead. It was quite a large Dragon, and it breathed a little thread of fire from its nostrils. By the time the fire reached the roof of the castle, it was a huge roaring inferno.

Sir Harold could just hear his Mother shrieking. He listened carefully. She sounded more angry than anything else. Sir Harold had every confidence in his Mother, so he tipped his helmet to the Ogre and kept going.

Sir Harold didn't do Dragons, and he didn't do Ogres. In fact, Sir Harold didn't do at all.

Tante Rouge

There was a man on the doorstep, hand raised to the bell. Hannah glared, annoyed, but triumphant at preventing the completion of that move.

'Well? What is it? I'm on my way out.'

God squad? Market research? Another charity collection? The man smiled winningly. *Not a charity then.*

'Good morning. I'm from Tante Rouge.'

Selling. Hannah pushed her way onto her doorstep, pulling the door to behind her, making considerable show of the three locks that must be secured.

'I'm not interested, and I have a bus to catch.'

She started down the path, noticing irritably that the man had left the gate open. The man followed, undaunted.

'As I was saying...' he tried.

'Shut the gate behind you,' Hannah snapped. The man obliged, the slightest shadow of a crease appearing between his brows, just for a moment.

'Mrs Brown...'

'Don't Mrs Brown me, young man,' Hannah said, in a tone designed to curdle a cow's udder. She turned her back on the man and started to walk towards the end of the road, and the bus stop.

Well researched, this one, checking up names before he came to do his pitch.

The man watched Hannah retreating, at an unexpectedly swift pace. He looked at his watch, knowing perfectly well that the next bus had been cancelled.

'Don't you young man me, Mrs Hannah Elspeth Brown,' he muttered, pulling his jacket tighter at the neck, feeling rain on the way. He was intrigued that Hannah was passing for a married woman, and yet had kept her maiden name. Besides he was not young, even by Hannah's standards, and was not quite sure he ever had been.

What had happened, he wondered, when had Hannah's life lost its excitement, its edge?

He had not really expected Hannah to recognise him. As far as Hannah was concerned he did not exist, had ceased to exist more than fifty years ago. He could not expect Hannah to know him, but it still hurt. For three years Hannah had been his joy in life, his reason for existence. It had taken a lot of work to find her again. Where was the girl who had laughed at making the choice between becoming a world class physicist or a successful dancer? He had been warned to expect changes, but this was so far from his expectations that he wondered if he had made a terrible mistake. When he was asked to choose, there had not been a moment's hesitation. Hannah Brown had been lurking in his heart and mind ready and waiting to be offered this opportunity...but not this Hannah.

Hannah's pace was slowing already. The man wondered whether it was worth pursuing her, whether there was the slightest point in following through his intended plan in the face of the stranger Hannah had become. The disappointment hit with a recognisable pain, but it would take more than pain to shake him. He pulled a rather dog-eared leaflet from his pocket and strode after Hannah.

'Paid by results, are you?' Hannah asked, hearing the footsteps.

The man laughed.

'Not exactly. Take this with you, read it while you wait for the bus. I'll be here when you want me.'

Hannah snatched the folded page and shoved it deep into her pocket, and sped up once more. The man no longer followed her.

The bus was late. Hannah propped herself against the only remaining tip seat in the bus shelter, trying not to brace her weight too much, for fear of making her shins hurt. She glanced at her fellow would-be travellers. A young woman with a tearful baby, two adolescents bunking off school, an elderly man with lungs that sounded like sandpaper.

By the time the bus appeared at the top of the hill, stuck at the traffic lights, as it always was, the queue had been swollen by an argumentative woman with three children and an anxious looking man with a mongrel on a string. And it was raining. Everyone was huddled under the shelter, trying to keep dry without any success, and the hierarchy of the queue had dissolved. Hannah just knew that, should she succeed in boarding the bus at all, she would have to stand all the way to the shops...

The second bus was a leisurely seven minutes behind schedule, and consequently, there was nowhere to sit on this vehicle either.

Hannah's day continued to go abysmally; the post office was jammed with irritable, wet, weary people cashing giros and pensions; the supermarket was smelly and dealing with a shoplifter.

The fluorescent lights made Hannah's head ache and her eyes burn. Struggling out into the relative daylight of the murky covered precinct, she sank wiltingly onto a bench. Her arrival was greeted by a scurry of hopeful pigeons, who had probably been hatched within the yellowing non-glass dome, and a bird dropping on her shoulder.

Searching her pockets for a tissue, she found the

leaflet. It would do. She scrubbed the mess from her coat and crumpled the paper into a ball, tossing it into a nearby bin. She heard a sigh from beside her, and turned to glance at the person sitting next to her. It was him again.

'This is harassment,' Hannah said frostily.

'Do you think so?' the man enquired, holding out another leaflet. Hannah shrugged, and thrust her hands into her pockets.

'All right,' the man said, 'I'll tell you what this is about: Immortality.'

'Come again?'

A smile quirked across the man's mouth – *no*, he thought of saying, *that would be reincarnation.*

'Interested?'

'In what precisely?'

'Not dying.'

Hannah was on her feet, and scattering pigeons.

'Don't be ridiculous.'

'I am in earnest.'

'Then you should be locked up. You've lost your marbles.'

'I don't think so. Would you like to sit down and listen, Hannah?'

'Don't you...'

'...Hannah you? And why ever not?' the man asked, forgetting, just for a moment, that Hannah considered him a stranger.

'Leave me alone. I'll call the police.'

The man squinted up at Hannah's frightened face.

'Go ahead. They won't know what you are talking about. You are the only person who can see me. I am here for you, no one else.'

Hannah glanced about, and collected a few furtive looks from uncomfortable shoppers, and a frankly rude stare from one of the market traders. Feeling suddenly weak, she sank back onto the bench.

'That's better. I'll do the talking, then, shall I? I have, in my pocket, a phial of the elixir of life, direct from you know where, special delivery, for you.'

'Is that what it said on that leaflet?' Hannah asked, unable to keep silent.

'Yes.'

'So show me.'

The man reached into his pocket and held out a small bottle. Hannah took it from him with a shaking hand. It looked like a sample bottle from a perfume manufacturer. Slightly under two inches in length, slender, hexagonal, with *Tante Rouge* in gold script down the length of one side. The liquid within was, appropriate to the words, red.

'It looks like blood,' Hannah said, 'I was expecting it to be gold.'

The man shrugged, and held his hand out for the bottle. Hannah found herself oddly reluctant to give it back. Her fingers curled possessively about the fragile glass. Her eyes met his, consideringly, and for a second he thought he saw recognition glinting behind the lenses of her spectacles.

'What do you want for it?' Hannah asked.

He recovered quickly, cursing himself for an idiot, and refusing to be drawn into an explanation.

'That is for you to decide. It is worthless unless you think it is has value.'

'This is some sort of trick, isn't it?' Hannah said irritably, 'you are going to start spouting religion in a minute, all about the immortality of the soul.'

'No.'

'Then it's some elaborate advertising ploy?'

'No.'

Hannah looked at the phial again, puzzled. *Tante Rouge*...it sounded like a guerrilla group.

'Politics?' she asked hesitantly.

The man laughed. Hannah smiled a little too.

'So: Immortality eh? Why me?'

'Why not?'

'I'm no one special. I've done nothing with my life; I've never even had a proper job. I'm a boring old woman waiting to die.'

'Not any more.'

'Ah. Hannah Brown this is your life ... do all the things you were meant to do, but never managed?'

'If you like.'

'Like what?' Hannah said angrily, thrusting the phial back into the man's unresisting hand. She was not about to recommence her dancing career in her eighties.

'Piss off,' she said, 'I've got better things to do with my time than talk to you.'

'Exactly,' the man said, but Hannah was not listening.

A wasted life, she knew that, and didn't need some jumped up...social worker...to tell her it could have been different. Too late now, unless...

...Unless it was true.

Hannah did not look back. She walked into the nearest cafe and ordered a pot of tea.

Immortality indeed. What was it supposed to mean? Eternity spent like this?

Half way through the hot but tasteless liquid, Hannah's eyes latched onto the pay phone in the corner. She could do with someone to talk to, someone sensible. She shuffled her bags of shopping across to the phone and fumbled in her purse for change.

She started with her daughter.

'Lynn?'

'Mum . . . Hello, what's the matter?'

'Nothing's the matter. I just wanted to ask you something.'

'Yes?'

'What would you do if someone offered you immortality?'

'What?'

'Immortality.'

'What is it? Some new perfume?' . . . Like Obsession, or Poison . . .

'No dear, eternal life.'

'What? Has someone been trying to sell you insurance? At your age? You know what Jim told you about using the chain on the door. Mum, are you all right?'

'Of course I'm all right.'

Hannah hung up sharply, so much for that. *Jim says* . . . Jim.

Bossy, tiresome Jim, who insisted on calling Hannah *Mother*, and asked searching questions about her investments, whilst his eyes flickered constantly over her furniture, her china. Hannah could practically hear the adding machine whirring – *don't like that, won't keep it. Nice piece though, that'll fetch a few bob when the old girl snuffs it* – to say nothing of his plans for her house.

Hannah shuddered. At least if she didn't die, Jim's little schemes would go to glory.

Hannah pocketed her change, paid for her tea and walked out into the rain. What she needed was objective advice, not self-interested opinion.

There was a young man busking on the corner, outside the Travel Agents. His spikes of straw blond hair were beginning to wilt in the drizzle, and his violin was going out of tune, but he seemed oblivious.

Hannah strayed to his side and gazed at the display,

unconsciously enjoying the cheerless squawk of the bow on the dampening strings.

Lord Gregory wasn't it?

Of course it was. The man from Tante Rouge guided the young man's fingers neatly through to the end of the tune, waiting for Hannah to make the connection.

Hannah looked at gloriously sun lit coasts. The Azores, Bermuda, Hawaii... she thought about Catford on a wet day and about travelling up the Amazon. Her passport was bound to be out of date.

The young man stopped playing, and tried to get his violin, no, his fiddle, back into tune, before launching into *Love is Pleasing*.

Hannah had learnt that one at her mother's knee. In fact it was the first song she could remember; but there were other memories to that tune, ones that should bring her head up.

The man stood beside Hannah, watching her face reflected in the rain stained glass, waiting for a reaction. Hannah stared through the glass, trying to ignore the tune. The man began to sing softly.

As love grows older, so love grows colder, and fades away like morning dew.

Hannah was suddenly reminded of the ice cold of her mother's tiled kitchen, in the brief period between the demise of the range, which had kept it warm, and the demise of her mother. She remembered at the age of four or five, happily singing of the disgrace and death of young women without the least idea of the meaning of those words.

Her eyes, no longer focused on the over bright photographs, met for a moment the reflected glance of a long forgotten face. Hannah instinctively turned her face, her thoughts, away.

I wish, I wish, but all in vain... Hannah remembered,

without meaning to, the shock of discovering her own pregnancy. She had wanted to die of shame then.

Hannah shivered and pushed her hands into her coat pockets, encountering the change left over from the phone call.

The young man stopped again, suddenly aware of the reason for his persistent tunelessness. He glanced at Hannah, who stood motionless, and apparently appreciative; transfixed by sun, song and memory.

'D'ye know how many different versions there are of that song?' he asked, hoping to jog the old bat into parting with some money.

'Yes,' said Hannah firmly, although she didn't. She could imagine there were a great many, having found six different tunes without trying, and stray verses in at least twelve songs that admitted to no knowledge of each other.

'What would you do if someone offered you eternal life?' she asked.

The fiddle player loosened his strings, and scrambled the instrument into its case.

A nutter, best humour her.

'Read the small print. There's always a catch. Loss of a soul usually, isn't it?' he asked, then catching the serious expression on Hannah's face, thought better of encouraging a dialogue.

Hannah watched his thin-legged lope take him into the pub, her hand still clutching the handful of coins. Well, he'd not be spending her pension money on alcohol.

Hannah thought about small print. She wasn't at all sure she had a soul, as such, or that she cared to keep it if she did. But what would she do with eternity anyway? Fritter it away in Catford, until some suspicious clerk at the benefit office wondered how come she was still drawing her pension and cut her money off, just to see what happened?

Hannah sighed, and dragged herself away from the glossy delights of Morocco, towards the Library.

There had been a time when Hannah had enjoyed the Library, when it was still in a relatively Library-like building, despite having been built in the sixties. It had still clung to the Carnegie model; it might have been concrete, but it still had a domed roof with skylights that leaked, so that you had to hop over the industrial sized mop buckets in every other aisle, and it had smelt right. The new library didn't even look right, not a single wooden object in sight, all plastic and computers. The shelves were laid out all anyhow, and even knowing her Dewey system didn't help much, since they'd decided to zone books – *Europe, indeed* – meaning any history, geography, travel, literature, biography, or cookery for any of nine countries might be just about anywhere on twelve shelves. Be that as it might, it was still the only place in Catford where she could hope for a rational conversation.

But Hannah's favourite library assistant was not in, so she had to settle for the eccentric old gentleman who was always ordering impossible books on, or in, Sanskrit. He looked as though he should know what to think about immortality. He reminded Hannah of photographs she had seen of a mummified pharaoh, Rameses, or was it Seti? The thoughts lay in uneasy proximity in Hannah's mind. Immortality, Sanskrit, and that ancient, antique head of his.

Hannah sat down at the cramped study desks, and fed *Immortality* into the computerised catalogue.

Not listed, the computer told her. She tried *Eternal Life*, but the catalogue would only accept one word cues under subject. Hannah glanced about looking for inspiration, or help.

Tucked into the corner as she was, it would mean abandoning the computer to seek out assistance, and someone else would be bound to steal it.

Rameses glanced up from his books and smiled. *Not his usual style*, Hannah thought suspiciously.

'Struggling?' he enquired.

Hannah nodded, trying not to look at the blackened stumps of his teeth. He didn't look that old at first glance. His hair was thinning, certainly, but not grey, and his skin was not particularly lined, just papery.

'What was it you were trying to find?' he asked.

Hannah had to clear her throat twice before she could get the word out.

'Immortality, hmm?' Rameses enquired, his long thin fingers flickering hesitantly above the keyboard, 'Theology, Philosophy, Fact, Fiction or Practise?' He wagged his eyebrows at her.

'I don't know.'

'Shall we try this then?' he asked, and input for Author, and then typed in, very slowly,

TANTE_ROUGE.

Not at this Location, One title found, press return for more information, the computer advised Hannah, but she was not waiting to see what Dewey number Tante Rouge had been assigned. Rameses hit the clear command, and glanced round, trying to identify the person who had set this in motion. He spotted him, passing the wrong way through the security system without setting off the alarm. Rameses returned to his books, sighing.

Why do they always pick Catford? He wondered.

Unpacking the shopping, Hannah stopped to put the fire on, she had not noticed how cold it was in her house. She had noticed very little on the way home, she could not get that tune out of her head.

. . . But that I know shall never be, till apples grow on an orange tree.

She plonked her bag of apples, unwashed, into the fruit bowl, irritably, and rubbed her temples, trying to get her mind into some other train of thought.

What's the use of immortality now? she wondered, *I'm too old to enjoy it*, she thought about the Sanskrit scholar and his appalling teeth, *And too poor*. Eternal youth and eternal riches now, that would be worth buying into.

Hannah smiled to herself, thinking of all the things she had not done, and would be able to do with infinite wealth and health and youth and . . . and I myself were dead and gone . . . All the things she should have done, if she had never met him.

'Hell fire,' Hannah exploded to herself, that blasted song, like a ghost haunting her.

How would it feel, being immortal? she wondered – what if she changed her mind? What if she decided she wanted to sign off? What if she was still lurking about when the world came to an end? Would she survive it, and in what form? Like being a ghost, always there, watching but unable to influence anything, unable to speak? It didn't bear thinking about.

Hannah fished in the bottom of her bag for a few string beans that had escaped, and her fingers closed over something small and cold. She knew what it was before she brought it out into the light.

The gold script flickered. *Tante Rouge*. Stupid name for what it claimed to be . . . *Aunt Red* . . . Blood red . . .

'Hell fire and damnation,' Hannah said between her teeth and set the phial on the shelf over the phone. For a moment she stood glaring at the glimmer of red in her otherwise colourless hall, feeling very, very angry with the man who had brought all her memories back, bringing all her choices into question . . . not that she needed to question them. She knew, without any prompting from him, that her choices had been wrong. Perhaps this decision would also be foolish.

Hannah went to the desk and rooted out a number of items, which included an ancient address book, her passport and her savings book. There was quite a tidy sum in the savings account, but hardly enough to last for eternity. Her passport had expired.

Perhaps the pyramids...Hannah mused, thinking of Rameses.

She looked again at the phial. *Ridiculous.*

One of the phone numbers in her book was for the estate agent who had sold her the house thirty years ago. The mortgage had been paid off finally and the house, as Jim knew, was worth a fair bit.

Hannah phoned the estate agent's number, and was pleasantly surprised to find the company still in existence. After a brief conversation she hung up and then she went to the front door. She did not open it at once.

Hannah stood with her back against the door, and thumbed through the address book, looking for the name she associated with that song. She held the book open and looked at the faded ink. Naming her demon. It did not make her feel better, nor even less frightened. Hannah sighed, feeling more sad than anything else. The name had been scored through years ago, Hannah had moved away, thrown out by her mother, and the man? He was long dead – nothing to do with her.

So why was he standing out in the street?

Hannah took a slow, deep breath, and opened the door, looking her past firmly in the face.

'Well?' the man asked.

'Tomorrow morning they value the house, and in the afternoon I go up to Petty France and get my passport renewed.'

'You're going to take it then?'

'Absolutely not,' Hannah said firmly, getting to grips with the future. 'I don't want forever, I want yesterday. I want the last fifty years, and you can't give me that.'

'Why?'

'Why? Because I'm an old woman, and it was you stole those years from me. I could spend the next millennium waiting for the world to end, when all I need is now.'

The man stared in incomprehension.

Hannah watched his expression change from confidence to uncertainty.

'You lied to me, didn't you,' she said, 'I thought you were dead, and all the time . . .'

Hannah's voice faded.

All the time there had been this . . .

He had sold his soul, Hannah realised suddenly, or perhaps hers.

She picked up the phial, and held it out to him.

'Here,' she offered, 'I forgive you. Now get out of my life.'

Hannah tossed the little bottle at him, quite gently, and with a reasonable aim, but he was unprepared, and fumbled his catch.

The bottle shattered on the path.

Just for a moment, Hannah regretted that little stain on her path.

. . . Oh had I w'ist when first I kissed
That love would be so ill to win,
I'd a' locked my heart in a cage of gold
And pinned it with a silver pin . . .

Her eyes met the shocked gaze of a man with nothing to offer her but damaged memories.

Hannah laughed; the cage of the past finally unlocked.

The Red Dress

Granny taught me to dance as soon as I could stand straight, and it is Granny I hear when I dance.

As soon as I stopped growing, Granny trained me for something else. Her black agate eyes watching me; fierce eyes: watching.

And now I am trained; I am honed to razor sharpness, like the tines on my comb; an assassin: I am my Grandmother's weapon, her gift, her honour, her absolution, her revenge. And I will be your death.

And now I am here, dancing, with you.

And I will think nothing but the tempo, I will breathe nothing but the cadence of my feet on the wood, and I will hear nothing but Granny's voice, harsh in my ears, always, always.

Keep your back straight, girl. Lift your arms so, and your back will curve naturally, don't lean, do you want to fall over?

And so I keep my back straight, feeling her hand between my shoulder blades, pushing. And I lift my arms, her stick beneath my wrist, this high, no more.

I do not tilt backwards. No, never. Nor do I raise my head nor turn my eyes.

Level gaze, girl, always, always.

And you have no idea. I dream the rhythms of this dance; I drink the wailing of my uncles' voices. You think this is a song, just one of those songs of a girl betrayed in love. Weapons do not understand love. But honour, that is another thing. Love dies. Honour corrupts and putrefies when it is damaged, and whole generations fall foul of the shame.

Listen.

The rain-fierce rhythm like the beat of my blood.

Blood.

Later, later.

I know about honour. Just one of those songs...

She hanged herself.

Yes, Granny, I know.

You feel the invisible bond between us that stretches, and bends and contracts, but does not break. No more than five inches, no less than one. We do not touch.

Other bonds, invisible to you, but stark and true in my eyes: bonds of family, of blood, of anger, of hate, bind you to me, binding me to my course. It will not break.

What are you smiling for, girl? Save that for your lover.

Yes Granny, I hear you.

We do not smile, no.

We do not break from the caress of that level, level gaze. I will not break under the strain of your ending.

Each step is a challenge. I stand here, and I dare you to break out of our few feet of space.

And so, you accept my challenge, meet my gaze; you raise your hands...so. Just the right height.

Granny's voice in my head

He's good, remember that. But you are better. That will not be enough: you must be perfect. You must win him; you must beat him at his own game. Do not lose your head, do not smile, do not invite.

I turn my wrists, my fingers playing you on the line, in time with those faint wild stirrings. I wind you in on that invisible cord. So, so, I wind you in. My eyes drink in the trickle of sweat on your temple. I do not sweat, Granny told me not to.

Your hand echoes mine, your elbow pivots, your shoulder turns, not a reflection, a symbolic relationship, untouchable. Back to back now, only for a moment, we must not lose the connection, eye to eye, an eye for an eye.

Swish:

The red skirt swirls about your knees for the second I cannot see you, keeping contact. We are carried by our momentum, back to that gaze, like magnets; and just for a moment you hesitate.

The wild cries of my uncles reach my ears, but it is not their words I hear,

Remember, Granny says, *remember who you are, remember why you are here.*

We circle each other, like opponents, like lovers. I am taller than you. A couple of inches, the height of my heels.

Stamp.

Granny knew the height was right, stable, better for the ankles.

Your body coils about mine about yours about mine . . . Your hand reaches out, fingers arching, passing mine; I can feel the faintest brush of air between our knuckles, but we do not meet.

Your hair curls damply onto your brow. Mine is swept back, tight, taut, not a strand out of place, held by the comb my Granny gave me, hard against my scalp holding all that weight in place. My scalp burns with the pulling of the weight of my hair, grazed by the sharp points of that comb. How I long to let my hair loose, to let its darkness swing against my back, but not yet, no, not yet.

The comb towers over my head. No rose, no carnation over my ear, only two flounces on my sleeve.

Granny said, Granny always said,

Three is one too many. It's your arms we want to see, not lace; you don't want ruffles in your eyes.

Red today, red as blood, and tight, yes, tight against my skin.

Leave nothing to the imagination, Granny said, training my body to the shape she wanted – teaching my muscles how to be desirable and whiplash fast and strong all at once.

And my body learned, I learned; and we pared my flesh down and built my muscles up, until everything was just so.

Oh, and the skin that must be flawless for the backless dress. And the ankles that must have the strength to stamp and threaten and yet draw the eyes...

Not my eyes. I do not need to look to know that everything, everything, is perfect.

Granny taught me how to be, and I am.

So our shoulders swing about the pivot that no one can see. And we do not lean towards or away, but we seem to do so, just as we seem to use the whole floor, but stay within that charmed circle.

No music now, just the rhythm of our own feet, that urgent stuttering, keeping time with our blood, keeping time...time for blood.

Down on your knee you go, and I above you, bend my arm above my head, twisting my wrist; twirling the line tight about my fingers, you think?

No:

I reach for the comb, for the sharp, two-pronged ivory knife.

Imagine I am a matador, my hands raised for the kill. All part of the dance, save this:

I plunge the comb so, like the matador I am, into the level darkness of your gaze, into the eyes that look up at me in horror.

And the weight of my hair, suddenly free, swings against the coldness of my back. And the weight of my life, finally free, flutters uncertainly in the coldness about my heart.

Blood red, that dress: perfect for the dance.

Judges

Well, what was I meant to do? Heber was off watering the goats, wasn't he. There I was struggling to get the damn tent up and trying not to knock over the jars of milk, me having milked the wretched goats before Heber sauntered off to the river. Anyway there I was, with this tent almost up, when who comes by but Heber's old drinking pal, Sisera.

Now we don't exactly get many visitors, not since Heber got so cantankerous and decided we could manage better on our own, away from the rest of the Kenites. He never was all that hot on family, a bit of a loner, except when it came to chatting up strangers at markets. You should see some of the shifters and losers he brings home with him, claiming them as life long buddies. There's definitely something not quite the shekel with my husband, but there you go.

So here's Sisera, hot footing it across the plain all dusty and bloody, so I call out to him,

What ho, Sis, old buddy, I says, who've you upset this time?

As if I didn't know. Always in trouble with someone, that Sisera, but you could hear the din of this battle half a dozen leagues away, so I knew what it was this time: that Barak, and the loopy Deborah. Nice girl, but her shekels were pared even finer than Heber's.

By all the prophets, says Sisera, am I glad to see a friendly face. Do us a favour Jael, let me hide up in your tent?

Sure, I says, but try not to muss up the bedding, your

clothes haven't been washed since last year by the look of them.

So in he goes, all panting and out of breath, even though the tent is only half up. And I have to abandon my mallet and play hostess, seeing he's a friend of the old man, and there's all that hospitality business. So he asks for something to drink, doesn't he. Do I have any water? Nope, Heber's bringing some back when he brings the goats. All I have is the milk, and that's already beginning to curdle in the heat. Practically butter already. So Sisera has to make do with that.

When he's drained both jars, he wipes his filthy mouth with his filthy paw, and then wipes that on my best Kelim. Charming. Sisera always was an oaf. However, the laws of hospitality made me bite my tongue and say nothing. And then he belches. Vile manners.

Here, Jael, he says, when's my old mate Heber coming back?

I don't know, I say, it's a long way to the river. We didn't want to park the old tent too close to the fighting, and he'll have had to go well up stream of your lot.

He looks all gloomy then, does Sisera.

Its a bad business this, Jael, he says, scratching his beard, those Israelites have licked me proper this time. I'm well worried that Barak will come after me. If anyone comes, tell them you've not seen me, won't you girl?

I may not be exactly an ancient wise woman, I said, all on my dignity; I may only be just into womanhood, but I do have some idea, I'm not a child.

Shouldn't have said that, I suppose, not to Sisera — one-track mind, that one. He gives me this up and down look, like he's sizing up my breeding potential and before I know it he's tumbled me onto my own rugs and is rutting away like the proverbial billy-goat.

Disgusting, foul-breathed, Sisera, of all people. As if lying with Heber weren't bad enough.

The rules of hospitality do not require me to bed any passing lecher who can remember my husband's name.

Anyway, I'm lying there, doing my best to fight him off, when of a sudden he goes into this groaning routine, like he's dying. No such luck, he's doing the other thing. So he rolls off me, with this happy little smile on his great mug, and falls asleep.

Well what would you do? I shook my skirts out and went back to getting the tent upright, with him snoring just the other side of the leather. I was getting pretty angry by now, as you might imagine, and somehow, his slime dribbling down my legs was just the last straw.

I still had my mallet in one hand, and a nice long tent peg in the other, when I went in to look at him. Sleeping like a baby, you could say. I've never seen the attraction of babies myself, nasty smelly noisy things, no use till they're old enough to help with the goats. So Sisera's resemblance to a baby did nothing to soften my resolve. I leant over him for a while, just looking. Not that I wanted to get close to him, you understand.

I put the sharp end of that tent peg against the side of his head, ever so gentle. He snorted a bit, but that was all. So I lifted that nice heavy mallet, and I brought it down such a whack.

I tell you, Sisera's head was a lot softer than the earth I'd been pounding the last few minutes. He never knew what hit him. Pity really, I would have liked him to suffer, just a little bit.

So then I went and sat outside, to take the air. Come over a bit faint I had, all of a sudden, I felt a bit queasy ...

That's where I was sitting, hardly recovered, when up comes bleeding Barak and his doxy Deborah.

She was well pissed off when she saw what I had done, she'd prophesied that a woman would finish him off, see, but she thought it would be her. She'd even brought a sword with her. So Deborah goes into the tent, and hacks Sisera's head off. Takes her three goes.

Then she says she wants to carry it back to the Israelites.

Fine by me, I say, saves me having to explain to Heber. You take the credit if you want.

I didn't realise quite how fed up she was with me. Deborah the Prophet looks at me all narrow,

No, no, she says, I wouldn't dream of it. You are a hero of our people; I will sing your praises from here to Babylon.

And she did. It was her revenge on me for stealing her thunder.

It isn't easy being a hero in your own lifetime. Plays havoc with your home life. You know, even though it's been safe to pitch the tent by a river for forty years since Sisera's death, Heber's never forgiven me.

All Hallows

Keith had a good view of the upper storey and roof of St. Gerda's church from his office window. When his eyes grew tired of the flickering of the computer screen, he would lean against the coolness of the glass and gaze at the worn, acid stained stone. If he squinted sideways, he could see the top of Gerda's head and a blur of burgundy red from her coat. Not that she ever glanced up; why should she? All the same, he gained the impression that she knew Keith was there, watching her.

He called her Gerda, having no idea what her name might be. His secretary claimed that this was a sign of insecurity; that Keith had an obsession with owning things, a need to name them, even the computer, which was called Maurice. Given this habit, the woman selling papers by the church gate had no hope of remaining anonymous. However, in this instance naming her did not satisfy Keith's impetus to own.

Keith chose 'Gerda' partly for the church, but also because she reminded him of an illustration of the girl in The Snow Queen. Bundled up in layers of clothes against the ice cold, her dark plaits on her shoulders, and that curiously angry innocence of the very young in her face. The illustration might have been of the Robber Princess, but as that character lacked a name, Keith had chosen to ignore the inconvenience of that possibility, and the newsvendor remained Gerda.

Keith passed her every day, going to and from the station. He used the churchyard as a short cut, stealing a few moments peace from the rush hour cacophony, before crossing the road to the office.

When it was warm enough, Keith took his sandwiches across the road, to eat his lunch in the slip of park which replaced the graveyard after the blitz disturbed the burials, astonishingly leaving the church itself untouched. If the bench nearest the gate were free it was possible, on a late lunch break, to get a little sun and to watch Gerda furtively.

She cut a strange figure, standing at her post and swaying slightly from side to side. She kept her eyes down, chanting that particular paper-seller's rant that meant next to nothing. One of London's street cries. All right for tourists, but a little affected to Keith's city-dwelling ears. He couldn't place Gerda's accent. It irritated him, not to be able to pigeon-hole her, especially when her voice was a constant in his working life, rising above the taxis and buses grinding down the road, to filter in through his open window.

Gerda never looked at anyone. She never once raised her face to meet the eyes of her customers. She did not converse, treating them with the same disdain they used to her. Like all the others, Keith would toss coins into the wooden clog that served as paperweight and moneybox, rather than press the money into her hand. Gerda never responded to comments. Were it not for her evident understanding of the headlines on the papers she sold, she might have been thought deaf and blind.

Keith's curiosity about Gerda was like an aggravating sharpness in a shoe, invisible to the searching eye or hand, but immediately present when the shoe was replaced on the foot. When he actively sought information, there was none to be found, as soon as he shrugged that failure away, his need to know would begin to prick once more.

Keith spent much time in avoidance tactics, taking a

firm grip on his curiosity, and turning it away from Gerda, concentrating instead on her name sake, the building outside which she stood for so many hours of the day. He was not altogether surprised to find that there was no such saint in the canon and felt, obliquely, that the woman at the gates was responsible for this intellectual dead end.

The church itself was equally unforthcoming with its personal history. Its age was unquestionably ancient, having survived not only the Great Fire, but that other ravisher of London's buildings, the blitz; but its origins were obscure. The available leaflet confessed to utter ignorance as to the original building, which had sunk so far into the marshy land between the Thames and the Fleet, as to provide the crypt of the present building, which in turn had sunk another four feet, necessitating a flight of steps both from the street to the churchyard and from the churchyard to the doorway, which was correspondingly low lintelled, giving Keith considerable difficulty upon entering.

Inside, the church was plain and poorly lit; the darkness caused by over-shadowing office blocks had won the battle with the meagre electric lights. The overwhelming impression was of cold damp moulderingness. The body of the church held little of interest to even Keith's voracious mental acquisitiveness: a few monuments, the font, and a carving in wood so dark and old that the features were indistinguishable, which claimed to be of the saint herself. Keith's inspection of this find was not assisted by the darkness of the corner in which the carving stood, and he flung ten pence onto the collection plate and took his peevishness away.

Passing Gerda at the gate, Keith got the distinct impression that she glanced up. He turned, but as usual, she faced slightly away, her head down. There was a dog sitting at her heels, one of those stringy, sad eyed mongrels. Ignoring the rain, Keith offered the beast a hand to sniff. The dog bared his teeth, and Keith hurriedly withdrew his fingers from harms way.

'What's his name?' Keith asked, automatically.

Gerda made no sign of having heard. Her rant continued, a garbled account of the front-page story. Somewhere in among it Keith heard a word. He laughed.

'Satan?' he asked, looking at the miserably shivering beast that was doing its best to get under the skirt of Gerda's coat. Keith fished in his pocket for more change, bitterly aware that he had fallen for the animal, as he always fell for them. He pressed fifty pence into Gerda's hand. She turned it over without looking at it, feeling the edges, accentuating the impression of blindness.

'For the dog,' Keith explained.

Silence.

Something of a reaction that silence, a break in the babble of newspeak. The fifty pence went into a pocket, not the clog, so Keith knew she understood. He grinned, satisfied.

'See you later,' he said, as she resumed her steady catechism of news.

Returning to the office Keith glanced at the paper. Something about ritual child abuse, so perhaps the dog was not called Satan after all.

Keith returned to the church leaflet, and skimmed through the remaining pages. The name was, perhaps, a local corruption of a more familiar saint, although the author had no suggestion to make as to whom. The current church building had a colourful history. It had been thrown up at extraordinary speed, using a well-documented gift from a local merchant trying to buy himself salvation, but the architect was a mystery. The building work had been dogged by disaster, with among other things, two deaths on site. The fact that the old church had been built on the site of a gallows was held to be the cause of this trouble and the site had eventually been re-consecrated before the building was complete in an attempt to fend off evil spirits. As a result the church had an alternative consecration to All Hallows, which was deemed appropriate at the time. Despite the consecration, the old name had stuck, and St. Gerda, whoever she was, continued in residence.

Keith's day ended late, after an interminable meeting in the boardroom. Keith managed to stay awake by drinking a good deal of coffee and taking an interest in reproducing, in doodle form, the Edward Hopper hung on the wall behind the Chair's head. This gave the useful impression that Keith was concentrating on the Chair's comments, and taking notes.

The meeting at last broke up and Keith forewent the possible joys of chatting with the Chief Executive in favour of a hurried scramble for the train. His hurry meant that he had not closed his briefcase as securely as he hoped, and, passing at speed through St. Gerda's churchyard, the case caught on one of the benches, and burst open, spilling papers in magnificent disarray across the paving stones.

Cursing, Keith collected the papers together, having to chase some right down the steps to the church door. Straightening from the awkward reaching after these papers, Keith became aware of a voice, muttering to itself. At first he assumed it was a drunk, but as he raised his eyes, he looked, for the first time, into Gerda's face. She stood above him on the steps, swaying as usual, her habitual hoarse rant softened to a muttering. Standing below her, in the darkness, Keith felt her presence as a suffocating barrier between himself and the safety of the station.

Gerda's mutter had turned to a lilting half-tuneful sigh of words, quite indistinguishable, but unaccountably alarming. As with everything he has ever heard from her lips, Keith recognised no more than one word in three. Those words worried him, although he could not think why.

Hunting . . . invasion . . . miracle . . . death warrant . . . plague . . . madness . . . disgrace . . .

Keith edged towards her, hoping to squeeze by, since she seemed barely aware of him; but as he came level, Gerda turned with him, and the light from the street lamp fell suddenly upon her face. Keith found himself unable to move, unable to look away.

Gerda's lips moved, slowly, as though tasting the words before she spoke them, and this close Keith began to make sense of her words, and to be alarmed the more by them. He began to move again, edging away from her blank stare, which seemed to neither recognise him nor register his presence. A calm face, he found himself thinking, a brooding almost animal quality to the proportions, and that strange blankness of expression that he recognised from somewhere, but could not place.

Suddenly Gerda's arm shot out, and her hand gripped him by the elbow, forcing him back down the steps, hard against the door of the church, her body firmly between him and freedom once more.

This is absurd, Keith thought, not knowing whether to be insulted or frightened.

Gerda's face was almost against his.

'Terrorist bomb rips through City Station; five killed,' she said quite clearly, and there was, for the first time a spark of emotion in those cold eyes.

The force of the blast threw them hard against the door, deafening and concussing.

When Keith opened his eyes, he was within the church, lying twisted against the font, with Gerda in his arms. He blinked in the strange light, feeling about for purchase to pull himself up. Gerda stirred, and hauled herself clear of him. Leaning unsteadily against the font she looked down at him, her long plait swinging so that the end trailed across his face.

Absolute silence.

Keith placed a finger in his ear, and shook it vigorously, trying to clear the silence from his brain. Gerda's mouth curved, not quite a smile, it verged on a sneer. Keith, feeling at a disadvantage on the floor, tried to force his muscles under control. His hands slipped away from him on the cold slabs of the floor. Gerda did not offer him any help.

'Help me up?' Keith asked, and found his voice distant and muffled to his battered hearing.

'No,' she said, 'I've done all I need.'

'What do you mean?' Keith asked, allowing himself to slip back to the floor.

'I saved you, I used my gift for good. I can leave now.'

'Leave where?'

'Here. I've been trapped here. Now I can go.'

Turning away, she wiped her hand against her coat, as though to remove the imprint of the carved edge of the font.

'Trapped?' Keith asked, thinking her brains addled by the explosion. She refused to look at him, keeping her back turned.

'It is pleasant to be able to say what I please at last,' she tapped her fingers against the font, 'they hanged me for speaking the truth, you know, merely because I frightened them, because it wasn't truth they wanted to hear. Not my truth.'

Keith tried to move again, and could not.

'Gerda...'

'That isn't my name.'

'What is your name?'

She almost swung back to him, but then she shook her head.

'I am named for the midwife of dreams, but I was cursed to always speak of nightmares. I never could prophesy anything that helped anyone. Always disasters, always too late and because of that, they thought my knowing meant I caused the ill luck; they hanged me, and they trapped me here with their church, the weight of all those stones on me, keeping me here until I used my prophesy for good.'

Slowly she turned back to gaze at him.

'And now I am free, so someone must think you worth saving.' Gerda's mouth quirked again, and this time, there was no question but it was a sneer.

Gerda walked away from Keith, as though he did not exist.

Keith watched the receding warmth of the red of her coat, seeing it as the only colour in the building, and realised what was wrong.

Turning his head awkwardly, he saw no stained glass in the windows. Pews lay smashed and buckled across the aisle; the pulpit was on its side. All this was clear in the unaccustomed brightness of the cold light through the damaged windows. Keith looked at the font, still standing above him and tried once more to move.

This is madness, he thought.

'Gerda,' he called frantically, abruptly frightened to be alone in this mockery of reality. His own voice rang clearly in the stillness of the air. The faint click of a door reached his ears, and he turned towards the sound. The door opened onto stairs, at the top of which Gerda stood. She did not look back.

'Fire,' she said softly, and stepped down. She seemed to waver in the uncertain light. Keith had a fleeting impression of smoke in his nostrils, and a great clamour of screaming and the roar of flames and falling masonry. Involuntarily he tried to cover his head. He cried out at the pain of the movement. Sweat broke on his brow, and he trembled like a hunted animal, aware of the sound of voices beyond the wall, aware of the scrabbling urgency of their searching, aware that he was the quarry.

Faintly, a familiar voice reached him.

'Bomb survivor found in ruined church,' Gerda called from somewhere out of sight on those stairs. But the church was not ruined, merely damaged. Gerda laughed.

Keith blinked. The roof seemed to sag towards him, and there was an ominous creaking from the huge beams. The other voices, from outside, were raised in sudden alarm, and the persistent scrabbling stopped.

They're going to leave me, Keith thought in sudden panic, and he began to shout, loudly and frantically.

As the first of the beams fell, Keith screamed. He kept screaming until the dust from the falling masonry prevented him, and all he could do was cough and gasp for air.

As the air cleared, Keith was aware of a great length of darkened wood lying over him, partially propped against the font, which had been knocked sideways. Turning his head carefully, Keith could see that the falling beams and masonry had barely touched him. He reached to give the beam above him a tentative shove.

It did not move, weighed down near the far end by more debris, but under his hand, there was no expected roughness to the wood, it felt strange, almost rounded. Keith reached further, and felt the length of the beam. It was not a beam at all, but a statue.

As the fireman lifted the first of the beams off Keith's legs, Keith reached to grab his arm.

'There was a girl here,' he said, 'she went down into the crypt before the roof collapsed.'

The fireman grimaced.

'Safest place to be, I should think,' he said. He turned to wave his colleagues towards the tower doorway, and the stair leading down to the crypt. Keith's eyes followed their progress with more attention than he gave to his own rescue. The inward collapse of the roof had left the stairs unscathed, and it was not long before Keith's eager ears heard exclamations as reports were passed back up the stone stairway.

A whey faced young man, who looked too small for his uniform, came back to report to the fire chief. Imagining Keith was out of earshot, he was painfully blunt in his distress.

'There's no one there, but the wall has sort of burst, there's bones all over everywhere.'

Keith swallowed hysterical laughter. What else had they expected in a crypt? But where was Gerda? Had she found a way out?

The statue was at last lifted from Keith's body, and the ambulance team crawled in to fit a collar and check Keith over before pronouncing him safe to move.

As Keith was lifted onto a stretcher, he glanced back at the statue; its face turned to the light for the first time in several centuries. He stared for several moments at Gerda's familiar blank, down-turned stare. The sound of her voice curled into Keith's ear, unblurred by bomb-blast, the accent at last revealing itself...

Keith leant back into the reassuring cocoon of blankets and straps.

...The accent of someone who had strayed no more than a couple of miles from Ludgate in all her life, nor in all the centuries since.

Déjà Vu

Lucy woke feeling weak, but no longer ill. There was sun behind the thin curtains for the first time in days; she could feel it on her shoulder. She pulled the covers up a little, burrowing into the pillow, preferring the warmth of the bed to the weak comfort of the wintry sun; not really ready to wake, not ready to admit she was feeling better, and would have to go to work.

Alister felt her stir. He turned to look at his wife, smoothing her hair away from her eyes.

'Morning,' he said.

Her eyes flew open, no longer half asleep, and a look of puzzlement and fear passed across her face.

'What's the matter?' he asked, laughing.

Lucy's heartbeat slowed again. Why be afraid of Alister? She rubbed her eyes with a hand that shook a little.

'Sorry. Still half asleep, I didn't expect you to be there.'

Not the precise truth. She had not expected anyone to be there, she had forgotten his existence. Perhaps she was not well enough to go to work after all.

Work? What work? she asked herself, the image of grey desk and filing cabinet fading into absurdity. Lucy had never worked. She had married Alister straight out of school at sixteen, looked after his ageing father for fifteen years, and when he died, they had settled down to having babies. Three so far. All boys, thank God. It was the only way to justify that long wait.

It was strange; she could remember nothing of those fifteen years, other than the basic fact of their existence.

Her swift explanation each time someone asked why she had waited so long to fulfil her function, her stammered, *Alister's father needed looking after*, was not fleshed out in her memory. She knew that Alister's father had been called Ralph, that he had eventually died of cancer. There were photographs of him in every room, so that she could convince herself that she remembered what he looked like, but deep down she knew that she did not remember his face, or anything else about him.

Lucy would not dream of telling Alister about her faulty memory, he might start thinking it was time to trade her in for a younger model. She wasn't doing badly really. Twenty-five years of marriage behind her, and no sign that his eye was wandering. A man as successful as Alister would not normally be expected to keep an ageing wife, it could be seen as a sign of weakness. Of course, having the children late helped. He would have a hard time getting out of their contract if he decided he wanted a new wife before Jonathan was at least sixteen. So she had a clear ten years yet.

Lucy flinched away from that thought. She could not get her mind to encompass the idea of not being needed, of being surplus to requirements, and all that went with that final dismissal from usefulness. Her stomach lurched again. No, she was not better. She crawled from the bed, and staggered to the bathroom, to throw up yet again. Alister made no move to help her. She washed her face, and ran a bath, intending to have a good soak. She hadn't felt up to getting out of bed for days. She really needed to get up, show that she was worth her keep. She glanced at her watch. God, she was glad the boys were only home at weekends. She went back into the bedroom, to get some clothes.

'Is that a bath running?' Alister asked. She agreed that

it was, staring blankly at the clothes in the wardrobe, none of which seemed to be hers. By the time she had found something she felt she could bear to wear, Alister had sneaked into the bathroom and locked the door. She threw the jumper and kilt onto the bed, fuming. She pulled a dressing gown over her nightdress, and struggled into the high-heeled slippers she found under her side of the bed. She took another look at the array of flimsy, foolish dresses and skirts in the wardrobe; they still didn't look familiar to her, or even likeable.

Lucy made it down the stairs, hanging on to the banister rail with both hands. It took ages to find things in the kitchen; the seamless sameness of the cupboards confused her. She made herself some coffee, then could not bear to drink it. She left it for Alister, and threw bread into the toaster.

Alister whirled through the kitchen, snatching the buttered toast from under her knife, downing the cooling coffee in one gulp, and was gone in a waft of aftershave.

Lucy wandered back upstairs, cleaned the bath, and put his pyjamas in the washing basket. She hated the smell of him, the way it clung to anything he touched. Not the aftershave, the underlying male smell of him, that even his habitual perfume could not hide. She shuddered. She supposed she must smell of him too. She sniffed experimentally at her arm. She needed a bath anyway. She ran the taps again, went back to the bedroom to pick up her clothes and search for clean underwear. She could find only absurd silky things that could not be intended for anything but fulfilling someone's sexual fantasies; not hers, surely, the knickers or the fantasies. Then the doorbell rang.

Lucy kicked off the slippers. She was not going to attempt speed on the stairs wearing them, not in her weakened state. She put the chain on the door. It was an automatic motion, one that she had never questioned, but she questioned it now. A half remembered nightmare rose in her mind to prompt that precaution, something terrible that she did not want to remember, or repeat. The half-shadow that she could see through the reeded glass looked small, but there was no sense taking risks.

She peered out through the crack of the door. A smiling face craned around to see her.

'Good morning Mrs Duncan, you're feeling better I see.'

Lucy's heart sank. The woman outside was the last person she had seen before she had become ill, and here she was, back again, the second Lucy felt even half-human. She smiled stiffly, and jiggled the chain off, so that she could open the door wider, there was no point in being rude.

'Mrs McCreedy,' she acknowledged.

'But you're not dressed!'

'No,' Lucy gestured vaguely upwards; 'I was running a bath.' Speaking the words made her aware of a gushing sound that was out of place; the bath was overflowing. Lucy wailed silently.

'Sorry,' she said, and made a dash for the bathroom.

Mrs McCreedy followed her up the stairs. The bathroom was not completely awash, but the pink pile rug oozed water where Lucy stepped on it. The taps turned off; Lucy rolled up her sleeve and pulled the plug out. She dumped the mat into the basin. Mrs McCreedy backed quietly out of the bathroom, put her small neat case down out of the way, and went to find a mop.

The bath replugged, the overflow contained, Lucy was determined to have her bath.

'Mrs McCreedy,' she said, 'I really need to have this

bath, I'm surprised you can stand to be in the same room with me.'

Mrs McCreedy smiled prettily; she was good at that sort of thing, she always made Lucy feel inadequate.

'Not to worry,' this paragon of womanhood replied, 'I'll make us some coffee while I wait.'

Lucy was not going to get rid of Mrs McCreedy, not now she had mopped the bathroom floor for her. Lucy nodded. It was as much as she could manage.

Lucy was glad to lock the door, but now she could not luxuriate in the warm lapping of the water, now she must hurry, and be out of the bath and dressed before the coffee was made, or be a complete social failure. She wanted to cry, but knew from past experience that enough salt tears would make the bubbles in the bath go flat all the more quickly. She washed her hair briskly. It seemed ridiculously long, and once it was wet, it seemed even longer.

Lucy dragged herself from the water and towelled herself dry, pulled a comb through her hair and made a turban of the towel. The flimsy underwear stuck to her still damp body in an unpleasant fashion. She wiped the mist from the mirror, and peered at her face, feeling resentful. She couldn't be bothered with make up. It was only Mrs McCreedy, after all, not wearing make up would be a subtle reminder to her visitor that she had not been well, and might not be interested in buying any cosmetics today. With luck Mrs McCreedy would take the hint and go quickly. She undid the turban, recombed her hair and plaited it. The plait reached well past her shoulderblades. She held the end of the plait for a while, swinging it to and fro, flicking water from her hair in an aimless fashion, then sighed, and hauled the rest of her clothes on. She did not feel comfortable.

Mrs McCreedy set a cup of coffee in front of her.

'Drink it,' she said.

Lucy did not like to say that she had not eaten or drunk anything but tonic water for five days. She sipped the coffee. It tasted awful. She looked at Mrs McCreedy over the rim of the cup. Mrs McCreedy had not touched her own coffee.

'It tastes terrible, does it not?' Mrs McCreedy observed, gazing placidly at Lucy.

'Are you trying to poison me, Mrs McCreedy?' Lucy asked, smiling. It was possible to say almost anything so long as she smiled, so long as she kept a veneer of respectful politeness. She had always known this, but had not been given cause to exercise her skill recently.

Mrs McCreedy smiled in return.

'And why would I do that, Lucy my dear?'

'I just wondered.'

'Are you still feeling strange?'

'Very,' Lucy acknowledged, allowing Mrs McCreedy points for that round, for turning her insult into a weakness. She was sure she had met Mrs McCreedy in a previous life. Perhaps she had been a sister then. Someone she had been close to, but had not liked.

Mrs McCreedy put her hand across Lucy's. She looked suddenly older, suddenly serious.

'And how did you take to the face cream, my dear?' she asked. For some reason, the question seemed loaded with portent. Lucy could not think why it should be so; it was an innocuous enough subject.

'I've only used it the once,' she replied, 'I've been ill since.'

'Well perhaps once is enough in your case?' Mrs McCreedy said. Lucy looked at her in confusion. What on earth was she talking about? This was not the persuasive seller of unguents that she was used to; this was not the usual game of veiled insults disguised as

60

small talk. This was a different code altogether.

'Tell me Lucy, are you starting to forget things, whole slices of your life? Are you starting to think that this is not your home, that the clothes you are wearing are not your own?'

Lucy nodded, not willing to speak. She could only think of clichéd responses, she was not sure of the rules of engagement, and in any case it was less effort to nod. Mrs McCreedy sighed, a great gust of relief.

'Tell me your name,' she demanded.

'You know my name.'

'Humour me.'

'My name is Lucy Duncan.'

Mrs McCreedy shook her head.

'What was it before you married?'

Lucy hesitated, her mouth starting to shape the name, then feeling it to be wrong.

'Hilary,' she said uncertainly.

'Lucy Hilary?' Mrs McCreedy asked. It would have sounded odd; even without the heavy sarcasm Mrs McCreedy dealt it.

'No,' said Lucy, searching the fog in her brain, 'Hilary Jenner.'

The silence between the two women stretched a little. Lucy could not understand why, of the two of them, she was the one to be surprised. She looked to Mrs McCreedy for an explanation. Instead, Mrs McCreedy continued her questioning.

'And myself, what is my name?'

'I don't know your first name Mrs McCreedy, all I know is that your initial is V.'

'Stop being so polite, Hilary, I won't drop down dead from shock if you stop calling me by my surname.'

Hilary. Lucy liked the sound of it, it felt right. Strange to have such a masculine sounding name, so old-fashioned. No one dreamt of using those sorts of names for their children these days. Boys' names for boys, girls' names for girls, should you be so unfortunate. No Leslie, no Evelyn, no Shirley. She looked at Mrs McCreedy, distracted. Why was she making such a fuss about their names? Was it because she too had an odd name? V... Lucy scanned her brain, Vera, Verity? But not if it were another male name. Vivian? Valentine...

'Valentine,' Lucy said with sudden certainty. Mrs McCreedy smiled.

'Valentine...?' she prompted.

'Valentine Robbins, and you aren't married to any Mr McCreedy, and I'm not married to any Mr Duncan,' Lucy announced excitedly.

'Not so quick my dear, you are so married to Mr Duncan, and have been the last ten years.'

'Twenty-five,' Lucy corrected; feeling thoroughly bewildered and tired.

'Ten,' said Valentine Robbins firmly, 'Ralph Duncan died in a nursing home twelve years ago my sweet, and you never met him.'

'I knew it,' said Hilary, a sudden surge of excitement and unusual certainty cutting through her exhausted confusion, 'I knew it. What's been going on? Why can't I remember?'

Valentine hesitated. This was always the hardest part, getting them to believe her.

'They've been putting something in the water, it stops you thinking for yourself, stops you caring about the inconsistencies.'

'Is that all?'

'No, of course not. You were brain-washed first, and they changed your name. There's nothing like a name for persisting in the memory.'

'Brain-washed?' Hilary asked. It was like some badly

written spy story in a magazine. Brain-washing indeed, where did she think she was, America?

'Why me?' she asked, irritably, 'and why not you, apparently?'

Valentine did not attempt to answer immediately. Hilary clearly did not believe her; she was going to be aggressive. It was hardly surprising; they had never got on. It was going to be an up-hill struggle, until Hilary started to remember more for herself.

Valentine rather liked to be the one with the upper hand for a change, to have the opinionated Hilary Jenner dependant on her. She liked being the one to have escaped the revenge attacks, to be in a position to help, not to be constantly in Hilary's shadow.

Hilary did not trust this woman, who ever she was. She never had trusted her. That was something at least, a genuine memory.

'Why is it I didn't like you?' she asked.

Valentine shrugged. She did not think Hilary had any good reason.

'Because I wasn't political enough, because I didn't take risks like you did, because I kept quiet and toed the line. Well, look what a lot of good all that shouting did you. It's not me who's spent ten years as a zombie, servicing some git of a man and having his babies.'

She regretted it as soon as the words were out of her mouth. It was no help using that as a weapon. She should be thanking her lucky stars that no one had thought to punish her in that way, not sneering at Hilary for being caught, for sticking her neck out once too often. Hilary raised her hackles. Shouting be damned.

'Perhaps if you'd been shouting too it would never have happened.'

Damn. Valentine had known she'd say that given the

chance, and she had, as usual, given her the chance. It made no odds that Valentine's protest would have been worthless, at the time or since, would only have served to make her vulnerable too; Hilary had hit the sore nerve, the guilt that Valentine lived with, in the comparative safety of her silence.

'I always knew you'd be around to write the history of the struggle,' Hilary said bitterly, 'I always knew you'd be far enough from the frontline to survive the war.'

Valentine cringed. Hilary had not had to stand by and watch, she remembered nothing of the nightmare; she had been one of the first to be re-educated, she had no idea what she was talking about. Valentine wondered what in hell she was doing risking her neck for this ungrateful bitch.

Hilary held to her anger, cherishing it as something real, something that fitted both the past and the present, and found herself slipping from denial to belief between one thought and the next.

Survive the war.

And there had been a war of sorts, hadn't there, and here she still was, alive, and in the enemy camp . . .

'Well I'm here doing the bloody underground railway act now,' Valentine snapped, 'so belt up and listen.'

Valentine found herself on her feet, no longer pretending to be that sweet young thing known as Verity McCreedy, finding her own voice of a sudden, in her angry self protection.

'You are beginning to remember, Hilary, because I gave you that face cream, right? I did poison you, if you like. It made you puke until you had nothing inside you but gas and bile. You've not drunk the water for days; the drugs are wearing off. So now let's get the hell out of here.'

Hilary could not quite remember what the war had

been about, or what part she had played, but she knew, right to her core, that there was something wrong with it being Valentine Robbins coming to the rescue, that was much more in her own line of country. She had never known Valentine take a risk in her life. Playing Harriet Tubman just wasn't her style.

'Just like that?' she asked, 'You have a car, I suppose, and a tame man to drive it for you?'

'Of course not. I'm not running the risk of being caught in charge of a motor vehicle. I value my hands, thank you, I'm not risking the loss of so much as a knuckle on you.'

That was more in character. But it was so important to be sure, if this were to turn out to be a trick, or if she was going mad, or if this was an elaborate way of Alister telling her that her services were no longer required after all...

'So?' she asked, playing desperately for time.

'So you get a train. I've got you forged papers. I stole some of Alister's things last time I was here, the paper and ink are genuine, the signature is a good copy. Good enough to get you past the station guard, anyway.'

'Where am I going?' Hilary asked, snatching the papers.

'To visit the boys in school.'

'I am?' she asked, turning over the second set of papers that said nothing of the kind. They were very good forgeries, if they were forgeries. What if she were about to be disappeared? What if this was a trick to get her to break her contract, so that Alister could get rid of her?

'No.' Valentine's voice brought her back to the narrow reality of her own kitchen for a moment.

'I thought not. So?'

'You are going home.'

Home. Then this was not her home, this was, as she had sometimes felt it to be, alien. Hilary had a momentary recollection of a tall narrow house with sharp gables, in a street of similar houses. That was real, she was sure of it. She stared round at the sterile purity of her kitchen, and hated it. There was no way of staying here now, with that reality lodged in her brain. She must go; she must risk the possibility that this was a nightmare waiting to catch her in its jaws. She must go home.

Home. More than just a house or a street, home meant something quite different to her. There was someone she had shared that house with, someone she had cared for. There was also a fear. She stared at Valentine, unwilling to share those thoughts with her.

Hilary Jenner, she said to herself, you are perfectly capable of doing this. All that is required is that you stay calm. You can do it. You have gone on a train by yourself more times than you can count. It is only poor feeble Lucy Duncan who can't find her way from one end of town to the other without an escort.

But the fear was there, the fear of returning to that house; the same fear that had her put the chain on the door each time she opened it. Hilary rubbed her temples nervously, absent-mindedly following the line of an old scar. The fear seemed to have something to do with that ridge in her skin. She remembered only sounds in the darkness, a confusion of movement; the strangest feeling of resignation, that now it had come, she could stop being afraid. No, not quite resignation, she remembered quite clearly that she had fought them, fought with great determination. But they had got her anyway. With sudden clarity Hilary remembered expecting to die. She had not died; they had planned a far worse fate for her.

Well, they had reckoned without Valentine Robbins, and her silent resistance. Hilary looked at Valentine from out of her memories. What an unexpected pleasure, to have someone you always thought was a wimp, turn out to be an amazon after all. Hilary pulled Valentine to her and gave her a hug, surprised at how right it felt to have a woman's body so close to hers. Not as surprised as Valentine.

'Why, Mrs McCreedy,' Hilary said softly, 'I do believe you are blushing.'

The train juddered to a halt, waking Hilary from an uneasy doze. She opened her eyes and pulled the blind at the window up a fraction. This morning's sun had lost its battle with mile deep cloud cover, and the rain, and the mist from her breath, had smeared and obliterated the station sign. She wiped the mist away, and suddenly realised she had reached her destination. She fumbled with the latch, flinging the door wide and jumped out. The door slammed to behind her, the sound drowned out by an irritable blast from the guard's whistle.

Hilary struggled with the belt of her coat, trying to keep her legs dry against the rain. It didn't seem possible to keep her balance. She wobbled through a puddle, searching her handbag for the travel papers, the ticket. Her ankle turned under her. Cursing, she shook water out of her shoe. She found herself staring at it in puzzlement.

What a damn fool item of clothing, she thought, thrusting it back onto her stockinged foot.

The guard scarcely glanced at her papers. Hilary passed through the dimness of the booking hall, and onto the forecourt. There was a taxi waiting. She thrust the piece of paper with the address scribbled on it at the driver. He took it from her, with a marked lack of interest.

'Papers,' he said. She waved those at him too, the second set, which said she was visiting a sick relative. Taxi drivers didn't have access to the computer records like station guards, he had no way of knowing that she had no relatives, sick or otherwise, here or anywhere else. The man handed the papers back and his eyes slid furtively up from her hand, to meet her gaze.

'Hello, Hilary,' Marion said in a half whisper.

Hilary made no sign of having noticed. She pulled open the rear door and fell in. Marion had the car off the forecourt and onto the road before she had her seat belt done up.

'You trying to kill me, Marion?' Hilary asked. 'I near died of shock.'

'Couldn't resist it. You always said it was a draw back, me looking so like a man; well, so now I pass. Comes in handy having someone who can drive a car openly. Need a quick get away at times.'

'But it's such a risk, what if you were caught?'

'Got used to taking risks a while back. I didn't fancy the Thought Police taking Caroline away to be a breeder, so we agreed, I moved in with her, and as far as the rest of the world goes, we're man and wife. I know, makes you want to vomit. You should see Caro in one of those frilly aprons, dear God, it'll make your hair fall out. Don't call me Marion, Okay? It's Mark.'

Marion talked fast, wanting to explain the crucial things in her own way, before Hilary got round to asking awkward questions.

'Okay, okay. Mark. How far is it you are taking me, Mark?'

'You don't remember?'

'Not yet.'

But there was something Hilary remembered. She remembered that Caroline had once been close to her, had shared that house...there was a sudden gap in her life, quite different from a lack of remembrance. This was a memory of loss, a memory of aloneness. It shook her, shook her to her bones. And so Caroline had gone back to Marion, after all. Safe, solid Marion, who could pass for a man if she had to. And now she had to. Hilary pleated the fabric of her coat between her fingers, an aid to concentration, or a trick to stop her thinking; one of Lucy Duncan's habits, not her own. Caroline...what would she look like now?

Marion twisted her head a little to catch a glimpse of her passenger.

'You know, I wasn't sure it was you until I saw the papers, You've changed, you've really changed. Its horrible.'

Hilary winced. She felt like someone from one of those fairy tales, one of those who disappear under the hill with the King of Elfland's daughter, and reappear, unchanged, years later. Except that she had changed, beyond all recognition. Hadn't Marion said so?

'There's no answer to that,' Hilary responded, irritated.

Why'd it have to be Marion? Why were they living this obscene masquerade, Caro playing the little woman to Marion's 'Mark'?

Better than her own little woman act, surely? Hilary wasn't sure. And wouldn't people become suspicious of this apparently heterosexual couple when there were no babies? She brought her thoughts back to her destination.

'How about you answer my question?' she suggested, unable to be civil.

'We're here, this is it. Your home, once upon a time.'

Hilary craned her neck to see the building. It was not much like her home with Alister. This house had a run down, sad look to it, quite unlike the shiny-windowed, frilly-curtained outlook of Alister's house. Hilary shuddered, feeling a sudden wave of relief that the house was not the same. She struggled with the door catch, and wormed her way out of the car, straight into a puddle. It was getting to be a habit.

The tall gables seemed to lean in towards her, not precisely welcoming, but undeniably hers; she recognised the depth of the shadow cast by the house next door, the way nothing would grow in the patch of ground in front of the square bay window. She found herself fumbling for keys in her coat pocket.

Marion thrust the keys at her in an embarrassed rush. It felt suddenly wrong to hold someone else's keys for her, as well as living with her one time lover, even if Caro had been with Marion first.

The lock was a new one, there were signs that the door had been forced at some point, there was splintering along the edge, gouges in the frame.

Hilary tried not to hold her breath as she turned the key, but it was impossible.

It was cold inside, cold, damp and wretched. The hall carpet was beginning to mildew, and smelt vile. The living room door was off its hinges. The skeletal remains of pot plants littered the windowsill. There was a trail of rotting clothes and broken china across the floor. The sofa had been stolen.

Hilary gazed around her, stirring the pottery shards with her foot. She knew that she recognised the house, but it was so changed, so desolate, that it did not seem possible that it could be the same house she had lived in for so long.

Marion stood uncertainly in the hall.

'We can't stay long, someone might get suspicious of the car being outside.'

Hilary nodded vaguely, and wandered into the kitchen. The windows were so dirty it was almost impossible to see. It had never been much of a kitchen, the ancient gas cooker was still there, not deemed worth stealing.

She automatically reached for the light switch, but of course the electricity was off. She wiped her hand over the table, ten years of dirt, but it seemed like more.

In some ways Hilary was offended that no one had thought her house worth squatting, but of course, there were no squatters any more. No squatters, no homeless, no travellers, no loners; no outsiders of any kind. Her house was too small and mean to be of use to a family, and that was all there was now, families. She was surprised it hadn't been knocked down to make way for a shopping mall.

The banister rail wobbled. It always had. That was reassuring. The bedroom was a tip. The furniture had been smashed, the carpet ripped. There was something that looked like a bloodstain by the door, a sort of smeared hand print. There was no need to put her hand beside it, to try the size. She knew who had made that smear.

Hilary headed blindly for the bathroom, feeling sick again suddenly. She retched dryly over the toilet for a while. She forced her gorge back under control, stood up straight. The bath had rusted through where the enamel had been chipped. She had always meant to do something about the chipped enamel, never got round to it, always too busy.

She turned, and flinched away from the looming shadow in the doorway, which detached itself from the wall and turned back into Marion.

'It feels like I died,' Hilary said. 'I feel like a ghost.'

Marion waited in silence, expecting more. Hilary did

not feel like sharing her innermost thoughts on the quality of hell she was experiencing. She struggled for something safe to say.

'I know this is mine, but I can't believe I ever lived like this. It's so...squalid.'

'It was rather nice when you lived here,' Marion said quietly, 'you had pictures on the walls, and bright rugs everywhere, and lots of pottery and stuff, and the plants...'

Hilary shook her head. The picture Marion was painting was true in its way, but there had never been much comfort in that house. It had always been cold and dark, especially after Caroline left. After she made Caroline go.

'I wanted to tidy it up a bit, so it wouldn't be such a shock for you, but Caro said we couldn't risk being seen here too often.'

'It's all right, it would have made no difference.'

No difference. Only Caroline here would have made a difference to this homecoming. But no Caroline, Marion instead. Hilary forced the thought away.

' Did the Police find anything?' she asked, assuming that Marion would know.

'I don't know. They must have found some things, it was so sudden.'

Hilary stamped on the memory that was trying to claw her back into the past, trying to bind her in fear. The sound of splintering wood...

'At least they didn't get the important things, they must still be safe.'

Marion was surprised. She hadn't been expecting there to be anything left. The trip here had only been intended to convince Hilary, to rid her of any lasting doubts as to who she was, to give her time to come to terms with her past.

'Where was it hidden?' she asked, caught unawares by the idea of anything surviving. Just like Hilary to have taken that sort of precaution. Marion could remember a time when she had accused Hilary of paranoia.

Hilary shot her a sharp look, but the sudden suspicion was as quickly gone. She tapped the walls of the bathroom gently.

'I had these walls dry lined because of the damp. There's a cavity behind here, full of papers. The only way to get to it is to pull the wall down, though.'

Marion grinned.

'I've got a crowbar in the car. It'll only be half an inch of plasterboard, won't it?'

'Won't someone hear?'

'Has to be done sometime. Better now than later, when someone may have noticed activity in here.'

Hilary nodded, feeling a quickening in her blood, no longer sluggish with drugs. Her hands were sweating. She was glad that Marion was quick, taking the stairs two at a time. Marion hefted her crowbar and looked expectant. Hilary held out her hand.

'It's my bloody wall,' she said, 'and my papers. I'll do the honours.'

It did not take long to rip the length of plasterboard away. She even managed to do it fairly quietly. She handed the crowbar back to Marion, and pulled the thick rolls of oilcloth-wrapped papers out of the hole.

'Let's go,' Hilary said, suddenly frightened, imagining being found here, like this. There were more bloody smears on the hall walls, that she had not seen on the way in, with her eyes not yet accustomed to the gloom. She traced the scar under her hairline. Hilary remembered all right, but she did not want to dwell on that memory, not now, not ever.

Marion let the car roll halfway down the hill before turning on the engine. There was no one about. Not much use for the shabby little houses here now. A sort of no-man's land, a battlefield deserted and left to return to the earth. All the same, better to be on the safe side.

Of course the safe side would have been not to come at all. Marion's mind whirled with the possibilities that had unexpectedly been offered. God knows what information Hilary had thought fit to hide. One thing was for sure; the escape they had planned for Hilary would have to be delayed. And what would that delay mean, in terms of safety, and in terms of Caroline's response?

Hilary clutched the rolls of paper against her, hands clenched tight. This was her past; all that was left of it. And not just her past; she held in her hands the histories, the very lives of all her friends. It was a terrifying thought. They had not been wiped out; she had proof that there had been a life before Alister, a life separate from men.

Lesbian.

Hilary tried the sound out in her mind. Mouthed it silently, feeling the familiarity of it on her tongue. Such a warm, safe word it had seemed once. Now it spoke of danger, a danger that her mind twisted from, trying to escape the memories of what it meant to be a known lesbian at a time of persecution, a time of war.

Hilary allowed her mind to stray to the thought of Caroline, her memories painfully sharp of a sudden, but overlaid by the bloody handprint on the bedroom wall, and the fact of Marion's hurried explanation. Hilary understood perfectly, some things could not be regained. Caro must be nothing to her now, no more nor less important than all the other women, whose names and faces adorned her papers.

It was a long journey, and Hilary made use of the time breaking open her cache of papers. A serious business wading through those papers, putting names to faces, faces to names. There would need to be lists made, of those who had escaped, those who were known to be dead, those whose new identities were guessed at, Marion would know, having access, as Mark, to papers that no woman would be permitted to see.

A serious business, but such a victory it felt, to have those names before her, to say to Marion, *this woman is a lesbian*, and to have Marion respond, *and this woman is safe*.

It helped to crowd out the intervening years.

So many strange memories. Hilary found herself laughing in shock at some of the pictures. An overlay of Lucy Duncan's way of thinking distorting her reactions.

'Did we really do that?' she asked, more than once, at some particularly daring stunt. She remembered the elation that had followed protest rallies; the anger and fright swallowed up in the adrenaline and laughter. Fun. It had been fun, even when it had been dangerous. When had she, or Lucy Duncan, last had fun?

Hilary was dog-tired, but so blissfully, painfully, unexpectedly happy; and consequently, afraid. It all felt so fragile, so false. So strange to be laughing with Marion, for the first time in ten years or more; trying to shrug off the pain of those years, trying to forget they had ever happened. But they had happened. Hilary found herself suddenly staring out at Marion from inside Lucy Duncan's thoughts.

'I have three sons,' she said, her voice over loud, 'Three.'

It made her feel as though she was drowning, the nightmare closing over her head, mocking her with its reality. Not nightmare, fact. Betrayed by her own body. Hilary clutched desperately at the papers, trying to make herself believe it had not happened. Trying to swallow her disgust, her fury. Marion kept silent, not knowing how to help Hilary.

'I hope we aren't relying on Valentine Robbins to get everyone out of this?' Hilary asked, knowing it could not be the case.

'No, she isn't the only one,' Marion hesitated, knowing Hilary's sense of responsibility, knowing that despite Hilary's sudden outburst, she had been hiding worse thoughts, ones she could not share.

'You aren't under any obligation...' she tried, wanting to see Hilary safe away, wanting to pay back the debt she owed, for Hilary having sent Caroline away at the right moment... wanting her well away from Caro.

'Listen to yourself, Marion,' Hilary said quickly, saving her the trouble; 'obligation, indeed. Of course I must go back. I've a list here, haven't I? Three women I could get to, three lesbians I can get out – easily, without anyone realising. I know them already, I pass them in the supermarket every week.'

... Revolutionaries turned into the quiet biddable women, who might smile vaguely at her over the packs of disposable nappies they were buying. She could not leave, she could not run away and leave women who had shaped her life, women she had loved, trapped in that nightmare.

Marion moved to protest, to say that it was not necessary, that Hilary had done enough, been through enough, that she could get away, be safe, that she must go...but she closed her mouth on those words, recognising her own anger and determination in Hilary's stark optimism. At the next traffic lights she turned left, and, instead of continuing towards the motorway, headed for home.

Glory, *or* Hope

I seem to have had my eyes shut for some time, now. I listen to the waves, quiet ripples about my ankles; heavy sucking roar further out. I breathe in time with the heavier sound – slow, deep. The salt kicks in at the back of my throat, replacing the thicker sharper taste that had been there moments before. There is the merest suggestion of another roar, somewhere in the back of my mind- lion or motor, or whatever it is – it fades. I clear the smoke from my lungs, the stench from my nostrils, the bile from my throat. Sun on my shoulders, zephyr against my face, neck, hands; almost stirring the hair slicked back against my skull. One more deep exhalation: Time to open my eyes.

'Hello.'

She stands beside me, looking out to the clear horizon. She does not turn to look at me as she speaks. I did not hear her arrive. I check up the beach; there are no obvious footprints, no shoes kicked off next to the high leather boots I had been wearing moments before. A little shorter than I, she stands calf deep in the water, once white trousers rolled up almost far enough to not get wet; getting wet. Her arms are crossed beneath her breasts, not defensive, but relaxed, the sleeves of the faded orange kurta also rolled. Her hair is not quite blonde, and just long enough to catch up in a band at the nape of her neck; hardly worth the trouble. There is a lot about her that seems marginal; almost this, not quite that. Almost beautiful; she is not quite ugly. She turns her head, and her eyes are – almost – the colour of the sea. Not the sea where we are now, a colder, more northern sea, is reflected in her eyes.

I wonder what she sees with her Baltic-grey eyes. Does she catch a glimpse of the raven's feather, the bat wing, the blue skin, the avenging trampling foot, the many armed, the blood drenched?

She is here with a purpose, but she is not the usual would-be hero, wanting my blessing, or to bring down my curse on an enemy.

'I'm Gloria,' I say, a name plucked from among many.

'Hope,' she says, sticking her hand out, and there is part of her lying, part of her that says that hope died long ago, and what is here is something entirely else, clinging on. I take her hand, and wonder if she feels the weapon calluses, the stickiness of gore, whether she can smell the other salt half-buried in the salt from the sea.

'On holiday?' she asks incongruously, but in some way it's an obvious question – I am out of place here.

'No, this is home, or it was once. I'm... resting. You?'
She sighs, shrugs.
'I'm travelling... a pilgrimage if you like.'
'Where to?'
'Everywhere. Every shrine and oracle I can find.'
I blink. That's a lot of shrines.
'That'll take a lifetime.'
A half grin.
'Several.'
'So why here?' There is a shrine of sorts, half way up the black cliff behind us, nothing special, some local shepherd type, I think; but that is not what I am asking her: *why me?* I ask silently.
The shrug again.
'I've been to Delphi.' I snort, that won't have been very helpful. 'She said to come here.'

'That specific?' I'm surprised.

'No, she said *get it from the horse's mouth*.' She pulls a tattered guidebook from where it has been concealed beneath her elbow and opens it at the page describing this bay, and the teeth-like rocks extending out into the sea. I nod; she's done her research. She closes the guidebook with as much of a snap as its wilted pages will allow. 'And, at Machu Picchu they said *talk to the organ grinder*.' Her eyes sweep me, head to concealed toe; thoughtfully, deliberately. '*You* aren't easy to find,' she says, 'I don't...'

I interrupt:

'Why would you want to?'

'...belong in most of the places you work.' She finishes what she had planned to say, disconcerted by an unexpected question.

Her fingers cover her mouth, fluttering against her lips, trying to trap words. The line of her mouth hardens for a moment, then softens once more.

'I have to put it right.'

I turn to face her, aware of the salt water rising slightly, dragging at the sand beneath my feet, pulling away the surface. I dig my toes in for purchase, I wonder if she can see the claws, whether I am trying to hide them, rather than gain purchase on the shifting footing.

'You can't.'

'I have to try.'

Something inside me stirs, whimpers, goes back to sleep. *Pity*. How could that happen? I don't ... She looks up at me, silent.

'How many lifetimes?' I ask her, wondering whether we have met before: whether I have looked across a battlefield, and seen hope in a pair of grey defiant eyes, whether she has looked out from a wounded warrior at the purposeful circling of crow or Valkyrie, whether the Morrighan scream has ever stilled her heart.

She raises her hand, the one that had been hiding her mouth, and touches the seed pearl necklace around my neck. At times that necklace is made of skulls, in this time and place pearls are more decorous, more appropriate, I am, after all, off duty. Her eyes dart from the necklace to my eyes. Does she see the blood welling in them?

'How many lives?'

I shrug away from her touch, shoving my hand into the leather jacket that hides my folded wings. I tighten my grip on my helmet – here and now a dome of black metal with tinted Perspex visor; elsewhere and at other times, winged also.

'How can you sleep?' She asks, but there is no accusation in her words. I glance at her. Pity, again. She pities *me*.

'I don't,' I say simply, 'when I can, I come here to rest.'

She nods. I do not think she finds much rest either.

The darkness creeps up out of the sea.

I close my eyes and listen: the mutter of sea on submerged rock, and the faint clicking of a gun being put together in another country. Time to get back to work.

'No,' she says sharply. I open my eyes and look at her, hard to see now in the darkness. She leans against me, her hands on my shoulders, and stretches up to place her lips chastely against mine – a soft, cold, virginal kiss; but how it fires my blood. My pulse thunders, drowning out the clink of bullets being thrust into the chamber.

'I have to...'

'No,' she says again, 'You don't.'

She places equally cold fingers against my lips, silencing my protest.

'What do you think will happen if you are not there? Will a hero die? Will someone who should have died, live? Will fewer children be orphaned? Or more?'

'I don't decide.' I turn my head sharply, free of her light touch against my mouth.

'Don't you? Aren't you whispering in someone's ear right now? Promising everlasting fame, immortality, paradise, victory, glory?'

I have no answer for her. I am not there, so no, I am not doing those things. But if I were...

She pulls my arm, disengaging hand from pocket, her hands are cold on mine, small, crushable. I hold her carefully. I let her lead me up the beach, up the awkward steep steps to the cliff top and into the near deserted car park.

She pats the Harley Davison gently. The Harley growls deep in its disguised throat, and grows back into the lioness she really is. Sometimes she is a horse, sometimes she has wings; this time the wings are tawny and blood-flecked. She huffles Hope's hand and purrs.

'Traitor,' I mutter, helplessly. Somewhere that gun is firing, and I am not there to guide the aim.

A courting couple glance furtively from their open top car, and I wonder what they see, how they explain to each other the strange barefoot procession crossing the concrete.

I do not know where she takes me, the lioness padding behind us, rumbling contentment as we walk.

We lie together, in silence, hands exploring, eyes closed. The gunman missed. I can feel his confusion. But now elsewhere there is a knife being wielded, poison purchased, and explosions plotted, I can feel it all, just out of reach, out of control.

Out of control: she doesn't know the danger she is in.

'Yes I do.' She says, snaking her naked body against mine. She takes the broad sword, the scimitar, the spear, the club, the stone axe, the knife, the rope; she lays them out of reach. Her eyes are open, she sees me, she sees.

So let her see – let her see me as I am, let loose, unstoppable, out of control... she laughs.

I blink. When was the last time I heard a woman laugh? Centuries upon centuries, and even then it was insanity and grief drove her, not amusement, not desire.

How can it be desire?

She strokes my wings, encouraging me to unfurl the full nineteen feet span of red feathers, the great arch of black clawed night. They come and go, the wings, like the lioness-horse; it depends on whose battlefield I feed.

'...Like an army terrible with banners...' she says, her voice a mere thread of mockery against the echoes of war in my head.

Her hands explore further, wiping blood from my hair, unlooping string after string of skulls from my neck. Briefly, *I* am a lioness, and that stills her hands for a moment. Now my skin is so dark it seems blue, and now so white there is no blood to it. She cleans the bloody symbols from my breasts, and they well back after her hands have moved on.

I sob. She stills, and kisses my mouth once more.

'I can't do this,' I say bitterly, between clenched teeth, turning my head away from her, trying to untangle myself from her.

'You *are* doing this,' she says softly, guiding my hands, my many hands.

'You don't know what you are doing,' I gasp, and she laughs again.

'Oh but I do.' And she does; twisting blood-lust into powerful, terrifying, simple, body-lust.

I should be elsewhere, I have a job to do, I have lives to end.

'You don't know who I am,' I protest, shuddering under her touch.

'I think I do.' And I half believe her.

For a moment, I can't hear the call of blood, I can't hear the raven's cry, the hate, the fear, the need; all I can hear is her calling my names, like a litany of deaths, as I slake her need, and she mine.

Nemhain, she calls me, *Agrona, Adraste*. I answer her, cry for cry, incoherent acknowledgement- she knows me.

It could be a binding spell, but nothing ever holds *me*.

Sekhmet, Anat, Ishtar, Azrael, she sobs into my neck, as my many hands discover her; *Inanna, Kali, Sàthach*.

Nothing and no one can hold me, not with spells, nor, as she tries to, with love.

And in the quiet after, she murmurs, *Nike, Glory, Victory*; as my heart pounds and dips in painful dance, unused to release, unused to this brief glory. Her face is wet with tears; mine, once more, with blood.

I cradle her against me, red wing raised protectively, against something I can protect neither of us from. Her pilgrimage is over; she has spoken to the organ grinder, the bone splitter, the blood drinker. She has heard from the horse's mouth, or at least the lioness's. And now she can give over all those lifetimes to some other goal – perhaps to sleep. I tried to tell her; but she thought somehow it was in her gift to heal, if not the world, then me.

' I was never in that box, Hope.' I whisper 'Pandora did not let me free; I was already here. You can't save the world from me... I will always be here.'

She stirs, smiles at me.

'How many lives?' she asks, 'Just tonight, how many lives?'

I listen. Turn my head to hear better. My raven-sisters whisper and croak.

'None,' I say, 'None.'

Hope nods sleepily, and wraps her arm around my waist.

'For how many lifetimes can we keep it that way?'

I shake my head. I can't answer her. I tried, I tried.

I feel sleep gather her, her arm growing heavy across my body.

I close my eyes. I can smell blood, half a world away; I can taste it on the tip of my tongue. The lioness murmurs, flexes her wings, removes the paw from over her eyes.

There are other shrines, other altars, other offering places, and other long forgotten battlefields for Hope to search. I have many names, many faces. She will never discover them all, but she knows where to wait for me, each time she thinks she has them.

I roll out from under her sleeping embrace.

The lioness stretches, dipping her head to the ground, front paws outstretched, a mockery of a bow.

I gather the arrows, the bow, the stone, the trident; all the other weapons she could not see. I discard the boots left at the water's edge.

Hope sleeps on.

I go naked into battle.

Starkridge

Starkridge nestled into the lower slopes of a mountain known locally as the Old Woman. It was a place for those who appreciated scenery, and were oblivious to comfort; the mountain was riddled by potholes, rough water and sheer drops.

If you had a good sense of direction and there was a clear day, you could see to...Without question a place to look out from, not to look at; a landscape with a sinister personality of its own, that might make the imaginative uneasy.

Totally dominated by the Old Woman, it was perhaps inevitable that Starkridge should support a thriving mountain rescue service. People were always falling foul of the Old Woman, she had opinions, and ways of dealing with people who crossed her.

It was not easy for a mountain to have a concept of time; but in the general way of things, the Old Woman had been around long enough; relatively young in the measuring of the cosmos, but ancient beyond all reckoning to the life that crawled upon her slopes. She had seen things, heard things, and drawn her conclusions. The Old Woman had a way of making her opinions felt, and ways of interfering when she felt like doing so. She was a mountain to be reckoned with.

In this joyless spot, beguiled by who knows what opium sullied fantasy, a Victorian playboy had built his mock-baronial hunting lodge. It was a modest building of only twelve bedrooms, a turret and generally gothic design. No one quite remembered what had become of this son of the industrial age, but he had not survived to enjoy his creation for long.

A series of short-lived tenancies had each ended in disasters of various kinds, and the hunting lodge had been empty for several years, falling into an attractive decay, when it once more became a centre of activity, and a new source of irritation to the Old Woman.

The new owners, the Randall family, had gradually recovered the hunting lodge from the brink of dilapidation using a substantial redundancy payment, an ill-judged loan from a novice bank manager and fanatical vision. Their intention was to turn The Hunting Lodge into an hotel.

George Randall had fallen for the Lodge's air of genteel roguishness and decay. Once the decay had been seen to, the thin layer of mellowed charm was ruthlessly excised and the Lodge was neither genteel nor roguish. It regained the eager, insensitive brashness of its youth and no amount of work or money could convince him that the house would regain the grace he had once imagined it possessed.

George had been fooled by the mountain. It was one of the Old Woman's mists that had provoked his romantic imagination, making the Lodge seem so sinisterly desirable. It was fortunate that Mr Randall could laugh at the crass vulgarity of the Victorian architecture, but in his heart he knew that the Lodge lacked that vital ingredient, atmosphere, with which to carry off its own peculiar style.

Paula Randall had imagined that working together would bring George and herself closer, that they would develop a rapport here in the wilds, with only their own company, that had been lacking in their previous executive existence. She was quickly disabused of this notion. She felt the Lodge to be a millstone about her neck, always making demands. She had done what she could to make the house comfortable, overcompensating for the bleak locale and draughty rooms by running the central heating almost constantly and several degrees higher than strictly necessary. Her chief ambition, apart from leaving the Lodge altogether, was to be able to fit secondary glazing.

Paula had enjoyed the renovation; she and her elder daughter had worked together, doing as much of the unskilled work as they could. She justified this as a cost cutting exercise, but would not have missed it for the world. Apart from the pleasure of knocking damaged plaster off the walls, it had finally given her an opportunity to get close to Karen. Working together, choosing carpets and bedspreads, there had been a semblance of the family spirit she had always hoped for. It had been short lived. As soon as the work was completed, Karen had gone, with much relief and never a backward glance, to college.

Both the Randall daughters deeply resented the sudden change of life style. Anita in particular, objected to being torn away from her friends to live in the middle of nowhere. To get to school, she now had to cycle down into the village, leave her bike chained up behind the post office, and get a school bus that stopped in eight more villages before eventually reaching the school. Anita had no friends outside school, and because of the transport arrangements, was away from home by seven thirty each morning, and didn't get back until gone five in the afternoon. This made home seem like a kind of limbo to be endured before returning to real life. She particularly disliked the fact that she was made to feel a nuisance when she was at home, and especially in the holidays.

Her mother did not intend that Anita should feel

neglected, but there was something uniquely irritating about a sulking adolescent swinging on the banister rails, or poking in the industrial sized fridges, when she was trying to get on with things.

Karen avoided her home as best she could. When penury drove her home, she avoided her father with grim determination. When he could not be avoided, Karen's conversation became monosyllabic, with occasional sorties into malice, covered by a layer of sardonic wit. Karen had grown quite skilled at this, tormenting her father, goading him, but leaving him nothing to hit back with. George found it difficult to cope with, and complained bitterly to his wife.

Paula could not see the problem. Karen's barbs were for George alone, and fell harmlessly against her mother. George knew perfectly well why Karen chose to snipe at him, and knew that she was biding her time, that sooner or later, Karen intended to ruin him in the eyes of his wife and the world in general. He knew she had the power and inclination to do so, and that he had provided her with the ammunition himself. His eldest daughter hated George with an intensity which comforted her.

Karen resented the way her parents had squashed themselves away into the back of the house, the attics, the meaner proportioned rooms, like servants. She didn't want to be a servant in her own home, and kicked against her mother's expectation that she would help out in the kitchen or dining room whenever one of the two girls from the village let her down. The idea of cooking breakfast for anyone other than a blood relation or a very close friend seemed nothing short of slavery.

Karen suspected that Jo and Meg deliberately left her mother in the lurch in order to make Karen do some work; as though they didn't see why she should have all the advantages of a college education and not work when she was at home. Karen constantly reminded herself, and her mother, that she was not being paid and that Meg and Jo were. However, the only way to avoid it was to leave the house so early that she would not be there when Jo or Meg phoned to say they were unwell. Not that there was much to do in Starkridge if, like Karen, you found heights, speed and small dark spaces difficult to deal with.

Despite her phobias, of which she was miserably ashamed, Karen had struck up a passing friendship with Tony at the 'Outdoor Gear' shop in the village.

Tony was a member of the mountain rescue team, the local information point for hill walkers, and the person who should be told when setting off up the mountain.

Tony was nearly three times Karen's age and sported a beard that would not have been out of place on Lytton Strachey or Karl Marx. He had a tendency to knit his fingers into his beard when nervous, then draw his hands through the hairy morass until they lay clasped across his stomach. He found this very comforting. Karen thought it looked odd. Tony did it a lot when she was around.

Karen treated Tony as a village wise man and fount of all wisdom and spent hours poring over the large scale map of the mountain which was pinned to the wall of the shop, under a large sign which warned: *Don't Mess With Mountains*.

Tony would describe the accepted routes, and some of the less acceptable ones, and the rescues resulting therefrom, in passionate detail. Karen felt as if she had covered every inch of every incline and sunk to her knees in every boggy patch, without ever having set foot higher than the modest contour line on which the Lodge was perched.

Within weeks, Karen could recite routes up, over and round the mountain in much the same way as a London cabby learning the 'knowledge.' Before long she knew all the unofficial local terms for the landmarks associated with the Old Woman. Most of these terms were derogatory, and indicative of the local wish to undermine the mountain's ominous presence with ridicule. Karen found the constant harping on the mountain's femaleness irritating, although she had to admit that in certain lights, the western face of the mountain did have a certain female quality.

Despite the local attempts to undermine her, the mountain was a mean place and most of the time she looked like nothing so much as a mass of dark cloud. On days when the sun managed to burn through, a heat haze would obliterate the views.

Tony, who had spent most of his life in Starkridge, and was one of those rarities, a local mountain enthusiast, admitted to having seen a really good view perhaps a dozen times in his fifty four years.

Tony could not fathom Karen's enthusiasm for the topographic detail of the mountain, he could see that she had no intention of attempting so much as a walk across the lower slopes. Given this, he could only assume that she was nursing some unspoken passion for his person. He was acutely embarrassed by this assumption, which made him gruff and uncommunicative. Karen took this in her stride; it made him all the more part and parcel with the scenery.

Like Karen, George Randall had never set foot on the mountain that reared behind his white elephant of an hotel. When he was not scurrying about helping Paula with the beds, or the maintenance, or down at the cash and carry; George did what he could with the meagre and unproductive grounds.

George had no time to go up the mountain, or even to think about it. He would have liked to have taken time to enjoy their creation, but the bank loan had to be serviced, and from the moment the restoration was complete, there had been a steady trickle of visitors. The Lodge had yet to reach full capacity, but no week had passed by without there being someone in residence.

Now, at the beginning of the second season, the week before Easter, which was early this year, there were already two parties ensconced in the first floor bedrooms.

Mr and Mrs Parry had the best room in terms of space and comfort. They were a middle-aged couple, and Paula Randall, who had a nose for these things, had them down as trying to rescue a rocky marriage.

Next to them, in a room which had good views, when there were views at all, were a couple of women, slightly younger than the Parry's but not much: a Ms Harris and a Ms Charring. Given that they had quietly insisted on a double bed, Paula assumed they were lesbians. It amused her to put them in the room next to the warring Parrys. She knew, instinctively, that they would dislike each other on sight. She wanted to see who would win. It was one of the few pleasures she had in life, taking an interest in the social interactions of her guests.

Davina Parry had chosen the hotel, knowing that Howard would like its pretensions, for he fancied himself as an architecture buff. She had been right. Her husband spent the most part of the first afternoon walking a slow circuit of the building, chuckling to himself at the idiocies of style and structure, clucking disapprovingly over the occasional carelessness of either the builder or the renovator.

Davina spent that afternoon asleep, a rare luxury, but she was so exhausted from the journey, and the weeks of argument and recrimination that had preceded it, that nothing more was possible.

In the next room, Fiona Harris and Ellen Charring were also in bed, but more actively engaged.

Fiona had more or less dragged Ellen away from her work, determined that this year they would have a holiday. She loathed London and didn't understand Ellen's love of the filthy street they lived in. Ellen hated the countryside, and had only agreed to go away provided Fiona found somewhere with a degree of comfort that would make it possible to ignore the outside unless there was an unexpected heat wave.

Fiona had nursed the hope that she might persuade Ellen into walking on the hills, but had been disabused of that hope within moments of their arrival.

Looking up at the cloud swathed mountain above the hotel, Fiona had felt her spirits lift in response to its towering magnificence. Ellen glanced up too, as she followed Fiona towards the hotel lobby. She looked up at the Old Woman, and met her, so it seemed, eye to eye. It made her suddenly uneasy.

'Good Grief,' she said, in quite the sourest tone Fiona had ever heard her use. And so, Fiona had put aside all hope of walking the slopes, and consoled herself with the thought of the constant availability of a comfortable bed, and the two hundred-mile distance between Ellen and her computers.

The rain started as the evening light drained from grey into darkness without the slightest sign of a sunset.

Anita, the holiday barely begun, was already fretting for her school friends. Paula was struggling single handed in the kitchen, muttering crossly to herself about the unusual regularity of flu bouts in Starkridge, both Jo and Meg having let her down. George was minding the bar and practising his bonhomie on the tiresomely opinionated Howard Parry. Having exhausted his thoughts on the Lodge's architecture, Howard was, with his third whisky sour, explaining his recent conversion to Christianity.

The slight drop in temperature woke Davina. She felt fuggy and over heated. A headache hovered. She reached automatically for her aspirin, her groping hand coming into contact with the leather cover of Howard's bible, which he had taken to leaving by the bed. At least he didn't carry it about with him any more. Irritated by the book's presence, she sat up and put on the light. She looked at her watch. Nearly time to think about a pre-dinner sherry. Not that it would help her head overmuch. She searched through her handbag for her pills, and swallowed two. Perhaps if she took a shower, she would feel more human.

The plumbing was unaccountably noisy. Hearing the banging pipes next door, Ellen untangled herself slightly from Fiona's sleep heavy limbs, and sought out the watch that lay on the bedside cabinet. Fiona's eyes opened.

'Where you going?' she asked in sleepy accusation. Ellen replaced the watch. Plenty of time yet. She snuggled back into Fiona's arms, and watched the sky darken through the as yet uncurtained window. She rather hoped the rain would keep up all week, then Fiona would not insist on going for walks. She wondered, with hazy interest, how long it would take to get bored of staying in bed, how soon her fingers would be itching to dance across the keyboard of her computer, rather than the curves of Fiona's body. She was pleased with the idea of a holiday spent doing nothing but making love. She thought that probably it would be Fiona who would lose interest first. All that scenery would haul her away and out into the rain. Ellen had forgotten the sudden feeling of dread that had struck her at the sight of the mountain. It was only a threat as a rival for Fiona's attentions, and not a particularly serious one at that. A pity Fiona had not chosen a classier hotel, one with room service, for instance; so that they need not get up to eat...

Distantly, Ellen heard a door slam.

Karen ran the length of the lane at full pelt, dodging the rapidly growing puddles, her coat wrapped about her precious burden. She exploded into the lobby, shaking herself like a dog, allowing the front door to slam behind her. Her mother, responding to the thud, appeared in the kitchen doorway clutching a knife and a carrot.

'Oh good, you're back. Those girls have let me down again. Help Anita set the tables, will you, love?'

'In a minute,' Karen replied, preoccupied with unrolling the huge piece of paper she had been trying to protect from the rain.

'Now,' said Paula, sternly, although she was already peering over Karen's shoulder at the soggy edged map.

'Look what Tony gave me,' Karen said happily, unaware of her mother's irritation.

'What is it?'

'It's his old mountain rescue map. He got a new one this week, he said this was too faded to be much use.'

Paula considered the rubbed and scuffed surface of the map, its pencilled addenda, its disintegrating corners.

'It's not that bad,' she said reluctantly, although she could see that as a tool of Tony's trade, it had perhaps passed its prime.

'I thought I'd put it up in my room.'

'Oh,' Paula said, faintly disappointed, the map had a certain rugged charm, like Tony. Like the mountain, if you wanted to stretch the analogy.

'Unless you think it would look nice in the bar?' Karen asked, mischievously.

'Not the bar,' her mother agreed, 'but it would look good by the door, it gives the impression that we've covered every square inch of the Old Woman ourselves, don't you think? Next to the tourist information rack?'

Karen turned to consider the wall. Very public: she would have to contend with the visitors if she wanted to consult the map, and it was her map, after all. Then it dawned on her. She had no excuse to go to the shop now, not with her own map. *Silly man*, she thought affectionately, *he still thinks I've got a crush on him*.

'Okay,' she said, 'I'll have to put it somewhere until it dries, though, or the pins will pull straight through the soggy bits.'

She smiled at her mother, shrugging her coat off.

'I'll just find somewhere for it, then I'll help Anita, all right?'

Paula nodded gratefully, and returned to cutting up the carrots. She hadn't seen Karen in such a good mood for the whole of the week she'd been back from college. She wondered whether she should have invited Tony to dinner yet, or whether he would feel intimidated by such an offer. It was nice for Karen to have a friend at home, even one as odd as Tony. She had felt grateful for Tony, once she had made sure that Karen was not nursing a passion for him. Paula nursed a passing fancy for Tony herself; he was so different from George, without being in the least dangerous.

In theory, at least, Paula would like to explore the mountain, and when she thought about doing so, she unconsciously included Tony in her party, and excluded George. On the rare occasions when guests set off for the day to walk on the mountain, she would watch them go with envy, before phoning Tony, to let him know their intended route, just in case.

The map ultimately caused something of a stir among the guests. The rain continued torrential for days, and individually, or in their couples, the temporary inhabitants of the Lodge found themselves drawn to inspect the mountain that was no longer visible through the windows, in its two dimensional aspect, pinned in the draughty corner of the lobby. It gave the strangest feeling of being intimate with the mountain, to know the names of the most insignificant of her outcrops and gullies. It was not an intimacy the Old Woman welcomed.

Davina Parry, in particular, was suffering from the enforced inactivity. The road in the valley was flooded, and consequently, there was no possibility of even a trip out elsewhere. Her husband had taken the opportunity to catch up on some praying, and had instigated a routine whereby he communed with God for two hours each morning. As Davina had not the slightest intention of joining him, despite his earnest invitations, she found herself feeling even more of a spare part than usual. This was only slightly preferable to the embarrassment she felt when Howard insisted on discussing his conversion with the other guests, or members of the Randall family. She hated him sometimes, feeling much the same about God as she would about a rival in love, except that she wasn't allowed the anger that would have been justified if another woman had come between Howard and herself.

Davina was considering a divorce, but could not imagine how she would explain herself to a judge, as

Howard would certainly not agree to end their marriage. And she didn't want to be alone; she just wanted Howard to behave like a normal, fallible human being, instead of this tedious saintliness. It would help if he would just be quiet about it, instead of telling everyone he met the 'good news'. It was so arrogant. Wasn't it the meek who were meant to inherit the earth?

Davina found herself confiding this to the Randall's eldest daughter, one morning, when she had been driven away yet again by Howard's devotional obsession. She had launched into her bitter diatribe before she had realised she intended to do anything of the kind, and found herself acutely ashamed of having done it.

Karen kept her eyes firmly on the map, reciting a litany of route markers in her head. Despite Mrs Parry's distress, it was absurd. So absurd that it made Karen almost angry. There were plenty of problems worth wasting that amount of energy on, plenty; but this wasn't one of them.

Karen stayed out of the way of trouble now that she had the option to do so; but still she conserved her anger in silence, waiting an opportunity for revenge. She was not strong enough, not yet, but when she brewed trouble, it would be real trouble, not this petty whingeing about God. It infuriated Karen to hear Davina inventing problems where none existed. What would Mrs Parry do, Karen wondered, if she really had something to complain of, if her precious Howard had abused her trust, as Karen's trust had been abused?

Davina trailed into silence, Karen's stony non-communication having finally impinged. She gazed at Karen's fixed expression, one that could only be described as furious, and wished herself a million miles away.

'I'm sorry,' she said, turning away, wondering what on earth to do with herself, until Howard finished speaking with his maker. She knew she had committed a serious mistake in confiding in Karen, and was therefore surprised to find the young woman's hand on her sleeve, restraining her.

Listening to Karen's harsh, brittle voice, hissing a few home truths at the flustered Mrs Parry, the Old Woman stirred from her contemplation of the water cycle, and shrugged the clouds a few miles higher, stirring the isotherms thoughtfully. Now she could see where to place herself, how to shrug off this latest crowd of irritants.

Ellen Charring, on her way down the stairs for a belated breakfast saw the touch, and was as surprised as Davina had been. Not hearing the words that followed, it gave Ellen something to speculate about over her Cornflakes and poached egg.

Fiona, receiving Ellen's version of events in a murmur of intrigue, was inclined to dismiss her lover's conclusion. She had seen enough of Davina during their enforced closeness to doubt whether she had it in her to leave her husband, as she so patently wished to do. Given that weakness, the chances of her seducing any woman, let alone Karen Randall, seemed absolutely minimal. Fiona thought Davina an extremely dull woman, and Howard a tiresome prig with some reactionary opinions, which he was likely to volunteer. She tried to avoid them. Ellen was enjoying her invented romance, so Fiona played along, and did not try to impress any reality upon the fiction.

Fiona had taken more than a passing interest in the map, and had held one or two conversations with Karen about possible routes. Fiona had been impressed with the young woman's knowledge, and had found herself casually dropping hints as to her relationship with Ellen, and Ellen's lack of interest in the great outdoors. She had assumed the blank wall that Karen threw up was protection against the thought of herself and Ellen, when in fact, Karen's reaction was to the idea of actually taking her topographic knowledge out onto the slopes of the Old Woman.

The Randall's younger daughter, Anita, felt that everyone was ignoring her. She moped about and did her best to avoid being asked to do anything useful, for being ignored did not stretch to freedom of movement. Due to the flooding, Jo and Meg were unavoidably stranded the wrong side of the river, and Paula was all too likely to demand assistance from Anita and Karen.

In avoiding her mother one afternoon, Anita found herself forced into company with Howard Parry. She should have known better than to hide in the conservatory.

Howard liked children, and mistakenly believed that this made him likeable to them. He considered himself an amiable uncle type, and liked to talk to 'young people', preferably about God, but he was prepared to consider other topics of conversation. Having cornered Anita, he proceeded to question her about her likes, dislikes, friends and relations in a manner he imagined to be polite, friendly and encouraging. This was not how it appeared to Anita, who replied in monosyllables to questions that she considered impertinent and condescending. She did not like to be questioned, she most certainly did not like it when, whilst chuckling over one of his own witticisms, Howard stroked her upper arm. She found herself freezing away from him, giggling inanely.

Anita never giggled. She scorned anyone who did. She could stand no more of Howard; she excused herself abruptly and made a dash for the stairs.

The hairs on her arm were still standing up, and she felt sudden very cold. Anita found herself wanting to talk to Karen rather urgently. A confusion of images crumbling in her mind, sparked off by the sound of her own giggling. She could remember once hearing Karen giggle, and somehow the sound went with the way she was feeling, the jittery almost hysteria that she could not justify. Karen would know why she was feeling like this, Karen would know.

How long ago had it been, that giggling? Two or three years at least, just after George had been made redundant.

Karen hadn't look like she was enjoying herself, she had looked frightened and angry and helpless. That was what giggles meant to Karen and Anita, a state of helplessness.

Anita thumped on Karen's bedroom door and walked in, half expecting to see that scene again; Karen lying across the bed with her father's hand on her breast, her face still and white and frightened.

The room was empty.

Anita sat on the bed, pulling Karen's duvet around her shoulders, trying to get warm. The duvet smelt of Karen in a vague, comforting way. Anita lay down, snuggling into the duvet, wondering what was wrong, why she felt so alone.

There was something hard under the pillow. Anita reached a cautious hand and touched something cold and sharp – a knife.

Karen was keeping a knife under her pillow? Anita pulled the pillow away and stared thoughtfully at the Sabatier that had gone missing from the kitchen the previous Christmas. All that time, she'd been thinking it must be under a fridge somewhere. Quite a long knife, the blade must be five or six inches.

Anita put the pillow back without touching the knife, rearranged the duvet and closed the bedroom door quietly behind her. No wonder Karen never let her mother into her room.

Anita dawdled down the stairs, keeping a sharp eye out for the dreadful Howard and hoping she would not see her father just now.

Voices in the kitchen, which meant, almost certainly, her mother and Karen. Anita sidled around the door, hoping to check on her family's whereabouts without being seen. Not so lucky. Paula looked up from her endless vegetable chopping.

'Make yourself useful, Anita. Fill the salt cellars for me.'

Anita made no response, going to the cupboard and reaching down the little glass pots.

The phone rang. Paula went to answer it. Anita stopped arranging salt cellars and turned to her sister.

'I just found that Sabatier that went missing,' she said.

Karen looked up from skinning chicken legs, her hand tightening around the handle of the knife in use.

'What were you doing in my room?' she asked, irritably.

Anita didn't answer. Karen focused her mind as well as her eyes. Anita looked ill.

'What's the matter?' she asked, already half guessing why Anita had chosen to mention the knife. She got no response.

'It can't be dad, can it?' she asked, 'he's down at the farm getting eggs.'

Anita shook her head, unscrewing the tops from the salt containers, lining them up, scraping against the metal surface of the worktop. She flicked one of the tops, sent it skidding towards Karen, then another, until all the tops were rolling about among the disjointed flesh of the chicken. Karen did nothing, waiting for Anita to speak, hoping she would do so quickly, before Paula returned from her phone call.

Anita tipped salt in the general direction of the little glass containers, spilling it liberally on the work surface, onto the floor. Her hands were shaking, but she did not stop pouring.

Karen put the knife down and lent over to wrench the salt bag from her sister's grasp. Anita resisted and the salt went in a great swathe across the floor.

'Bastards,' Anita said, conversationally, 'fucking bastards.'

She knocked a few of the glass pots onto the floor. They bounced.

Anita sighed, disappointed at the lack of destruction. She picked the pots up again, stirring the salt with her foot.

'Yes,' Karen said, fetching the dustpan and brush.

Karen did not offer to sweep up the salt. She scraped the clean salt from the table into the containers, and resealed them.

There was a knock, and Ellen Charring put her head round the door.

'Oh,' she said observing the mess.

'I dropped it,' Anita said,

'We were fighting,' Karen said.

Ellen looked from one to the other.

'None of my business, is it?' she said, sensing that they might like to make it her business. Anita looked like she was in shock, and Karen was distinctly tight-lipped and wild of eye.

'I just dropped by to let you know your mother's had to go and pick your father up, the van's broken down.'

'Again,' the Randalls chorused.

'Yeah, well, gives you time to clear up. Do you want a hand?'

At some point in the cleaning, and subsequent amiable assistance with cooking, Ellen picked up the crucial points of the story that the Randall girls were not quite telling her, hedging about their explanations with a vagueness that did nothing to disguise the reality. Anita had been quite blunt about Howard Parry.

Bloody hypocrite, Ellen thought, guessing at what he thought of her own sexuality. It took very little imagination to make the connections between his behaviour and the tight-lipped warning glance Karen had given when Anita said something about her father. Ellen had been brought up on folk tales, she knew all about salt.

Ellen made herself scarce as she heard the distant thud of the back door.

Fiona could not understand why Ellen had turned so suddenly sour. She had spent nearly an hour somewhere that she would not discuss, and now she would scarcely speak. Ellen stared fixedly out of the window, at the rain sodden front lawn, which was all that could be seen, a deep frown marring her usually serene face; brooding, angry.

The following morning, Ellen woke unusually early, for her. She lay listening to the distant sound of tables being laid. She wondered which of the Randalls had this task this morning. She thought about Karen, laying knives out, carefully straight, a precise distance from the edge of the table; of Anita and her salt cellars, carelessly dumped somewhere within reach should they be needed. She thought about George Randall...Ellen got out of bed and pulled back the heavy curtains.

The Old Woman had made a pact with the weather front. The rain had stopped. More than this, the sun was making a weak attempt at turning the sky into something attractive. Ellen felt a great relief, as though the cloud cover had been banished from her brain as well as the mountain. She let the sunlight enter her limbs, and felt a sudden urgent energy, a desire to be out and away from the claustrophobic darkness of the Lodge. She flung herself back to the bed, jolting Fiona awake.

'Come on,' she said, pulling at Fiona's inert limbs, 'get your walking gear on, the Old Woman's decided to smile for a change. I want to go look at this famous view before the fog hits again.'

Davina felt pained by the noisy enthusiasm of the younger women, stoking up on extra rounds of toast, poring over their map. She glanced at Howard over the rim of her teacup. She imagined he must also feel the sudden release from tension presaged by the sun that streamed into the dining room. She wanted to get out into the warm air, get some real space about her. Not that she was a great one for the concept of walking, but she did not imagine that the flood would have subsided sufficiently for any alternative entertainment.

Howard smiled placidly at the younger Randall girl. Her eyes slid away from him, and she took a circuitous route back to the kitchen, putting another table between them. He sighed; he just didn't understand teenagers. He poured more coffee, and took his cup through to the hall to glance over the mountain map. He knew that Davina would consider his carrying a cup around poor manners and she no doubt expected him to either spill the coffee, or leave the cup somewhere inconsiderate; but then she always treated him like an ill mannered nine year old.

Paula found Mr Parry peering at the map, knees awkwardly bent, to get a good look at one of the lower portions. She offered him one of the walking maps. He took it graciously, put the coffee cup down on the bottom stair, and took the map into the bar, where he could lay it out on a table. Paula took the cup back to the kitchen.

Howard found what he was looking for. He folded the map carefully, with the required portion outermost, and carried it in triumph to his wife.

Davina noticed the lack of coffee cup, but refrained from comment. Howard placed the map before her, and pointed out a ruined chapel a few miles up one of the better-marked routes on the Old Woman. Davina sighed. Of course, they would walk there. Architecture and God ensured Howard would be happy. She could look at the view, if it materialised, and try to wipe Karen Randall's angry words from her mind with the sun soaked scenery. She ought to be glad, as Karen had told her, that her only problem was an excess of God.

Paula Randall cleared her throat; she was out of the practice of having to make this announcement.

'If any guests are intending to walk on the mountain, please let me know your route, just as a safety precaution.'

She was greeted by a momentary silence, then Mr Parry announced his intentions. She noticed an irritated glance pass between her other guests. The two women bent once more over their map, and after a brief discussion, proposed a route taking the opposite direction to Mr Parry.

Paula was looking forward to not having the guests under her feet. Life went so much smoother when the Lodge was unencumbered. She would be able to vacuum the stairs. But first she must phone Tony, and then perhaps she could take a turn through the grounds.

While she was on the phone, Paula saw Ms Charring

and her friend leave, sensibly dressed, rainwear tucked into the straps of the rucksack Ellen was carrying.

Tony sounded unusually cheerful, and told her that the river had gone down appreciably in the night, and that the road should be passable by evening, so long as there was no more rain. Paula had given up listening to weather forecasts; they never bore any relation to what actually happened this far up the mountain.

'Is there likely to be more rain?' she asked.

'Probably. The pressure is still very low, for all this little burst of sun. This is just one of the Old Woman's quirks. Anyway, Paula, what was it you were phoning about?'

Paula explained, and listened to Tony's absent-minded humming as he stuck pins into his map.

'I shouldn't worry they'll get wet,' he observed, 'hardly going any distance either lot of them. They'll be back long before the rain hits, if it does.'

Reassured, Paula hung up and went to walk the gravel paths, and smell the wet earth and dripping Rhododendron leaves. She saw the Parrys leaving from a distance. Mrs Parry was wearing a skirt and jacket that Paula considered more appropriate for a trip to the cinema than a walk on any mountain, especially this one.

Some people just have no idea, she thought irritably.

Returning to the kitchen, Paula kicked off her boots in the back porch. She was lacing her shoes, when she heard voices raised. George having another row with Karen, she supposed. Why couldn't they leave each other alone?

Karen came storming through the hall at full tilt. Paula thought about calling her back, but couldn't summon the energy.

There was a crash from the kitchen. Paula pushed

through the door ready to do battle. A small projectile whizzed past her, smashing against the wall. She ducked.

Anita stopped throwing salt cellars. George leapt forward and grabbed her, picking her up bodily so that her feet no longer reached the floor. Anita squirmed, sobbing and dug her nails into his arm as hard as she could, drawing blood.

'What the hell is going on?' Paula screamed, over George's cursing, and Anita's hysterical sobbing.

George let go for long enough to hit Anita, long enough for her to land a sharp kick to his shin, and run past her mother, out of the kitchen.

George ran the cold tap on his wound, splashing blood on the draining board. Paula reached automatically for a cloth to mop it up.

'Do I get an explanation?' she asked.

George dabbed at the scratches.

'I think both our daughters have P.M.T,' he said.

Paula slammed the cloth onto the side of the sink. She knew for a fact that Anita was not pre-menstrual, and she hated it when George blamed her own, perfectly reasonable temper, on her hormones.

'I don't think so,' she said sharply.

'Must be the weather then.'

Paula grunted disbelievingly.

'What have you done to upset them both in such quick succession?'

George met her eyes.

'I have not the slightest idea,' he said earnestly.

Paula knew he was lying, but that she would have to ask the girls if she wanted to know what had been the cause of the fight.

'Well, you needn't think I'm clearing up all this glass,' she said, hauling the broom from the cupboard.

When she turned, George had gone, only the faint swinging of the door betraying his passing.

Paula swept up the glass. From the number of little plastic caps, Anita had been throwing salt cellars for some time.

The rain clouds gathered shortly after twelve. They crept, darkening, down the sky until they were settled on the uppermost peaks, the edges bleeding like deliquescent mushrooms, spilling cold onto the suddenly yellow sky. The Old Woman pulled her icy cloak about her with every sign of satisfaction. The Parrys really ought to have thought about why that chapel was a ruin. The Old Woman didn't hold with Christianity.

At about two, Paula glanced anxiously at the vanished scenery, at the grey wall pressing down around the house. She turned off the radio and listened. Apart from the hum of the refrigerators, the Lodge was silent. The rain filled her ears as a dull, incessant roaring. Her family and guests were scattered, who knew where on the mountainside, and she was alone in a house she had never felt was home. Automatically she reached for the central heating controls, which she shot to maximum and then for the phone.

Tony was, as Paula had hoped, extremely calm. This allowed her to be as unreasonable as she wanted, without the slightest fear of having her terror confirmed. Tony pointed out that her guests had not gone far, and had maps, and that Karen knew the mountain like the back of her hand. He listened to the tremor in Paula's voice diminish, and looked through the plate glass window of the shop, at the water that was pouring off the tattered canopy to join the raging torrent that had been a street a moment before. As he spoke, he pulled the list of Mountain Rescue volunteers towards him, and checked once more on the small red pins in his brand new map.

'Okay, Paula,' he said, 'why don't you put a pan of soup on the stove, and I'll come over to keep you company until those idiot children of yours stop sulking and come home cold and wet.'

There was no point her worrying while she was there on her own. As soon as Paula had hung up, Tony started dialling the first number on his list.

Fiona hadn't noticed the rain clouds gathering behind them, she had been too engrossed in Ellen, and the charms of making love al fresco, sheltered by the rock outcrop known locally as The Old Woman's Tits.

Ellen had been persuaded by a view over three counties; and consequently, there being not the slightest chance of being surprised by any enterprising hill walker.

Neither of them had had the slightest intention of indulging themselves in this fashion, but the sun had lifted Ellen's spirits, and she felt she had been giving Fiona an unreasonably hard time of late. Fiona, likewise, had felt better for some exercise, and it had only been when they clambered up here to be out of the wind and admire the view, that the cosiness of her arms about Ellen had quickened into something altogether unexpected.

The Old Woman was surprised too. This was not the usual behaviour of her unwelcome visitors. She decided she was flattered, she hadn't had this kind of thing happen in centuries. Not that it stopped her carrying out her plans.

The view was no longer in evidence, and the cold seeping out of the rocks was suddenly intensified by large drops of rain.

'Shit,' Ellen said, quite cheerfully, as she struggled to

get her bright yellow cagoule untangled from the straps of the rucksack.

Fiona shivered, and looked up anxiously. The sky did not look as though it planned to drop a short shower and pass on.

'I think maybe we should get back down to the track before this gets any worse,' she suggested.

By the time they reached the relatively level track, the rain was blinding, and all that could be seen of their rocky retreat was a dark mass of cloud.

I'm frightened, Fiona thought, in surprise.

Ellen looked hunched and cold, but seemed entirely happy to let Fiona lead the way, confident that she was capable of doing so. Fiona was not so sure. The ground in places had been very muddy, and some of the climbs had been steep. In conditions like this, those climbs would be dangerous; they could slip and hurt themselves. She felt her chest tightening at the thought, beginning to allow panic into her thoughts. To wander off the path would be insane, there were no land marks visible. They would have to inch their way down off the mountain, or find somewhere sheltered to wait out the rain, always supposing it stopped.

Fiona hitched the rucksack higher and grabbed Ellen's hand. Water was running straight off the bottom of her cagoule, drenching her legs. She was already cold. There was water in her pockets, for god's sake.

Keep calm, she told herself, wishing she had had the forethought to get a plastic cover for the map. She set off along the track, Ellen's hand tightly grasped. Barely able to see more than a few feet ahead, she watched instead for the footing. Ellen stumbled trustingly behind, her faith in Fiona's ability to find the way back unwavering.

Davina Parry was furious. Not only had the ruined

chapel turned out to be a heap of rubble that could as easily have been a cowshed, but now it had started raining, at the optimum point from any sign of shelter. What had started out as a pleasant stroll through early spring sunshine had turned into a nightmare.

She was already drenched to the skin, and Howard had now started to sing, of all things. Fortunately the roar of the pounding rain drowned out most of the words. However, she recognised enough to know that it was something about rain falling on the righteous as well as the ungodly. A pity God was so impartial, she thought angrily, as her ankle twisted under her again.

Davina glared at the rapidly disintegrating map in her hand, trying to make out which of the alternative left turns marked on it related to the one she had just made out. She did not want to end up in one of the disused quarries, although perhaps they might provide some shelter. She turned to consult Howard. He seemed supremely unconcerned, and scarcely glanced at the map.

'This one will do,' he said cheerfully.

Davina peered once more at the map. As far as she could remember, they had already passed the turning that skirted the top of the quarry. She tucked the map under her jacket, in the faint hope of protecting it a little, and set off along the track, Howard humming in her wake.

There were several Landrovers in the drive. Paula felt her knees give a little: Tony was taking her seriously after all. She opened the door, and made way for the small knots of men to rush from their vehicles to the lobby of the Lodge. The knots dissolved into individuals and Tony stepped towards her.

'Didn't want you worrying,' he said.

Paula made a dismissive movement with her hand,

completely unable to speak for a moment.

'Do you have any idea where the girls would have gone?' Tony asked.

Paula shook her head and tried to work out which muscles controlled her vocal cords.

'They'd been fighting with George,' she said, 'all three of them just charged off, no coats, nothing.'

Michael, who owned the garage, grimaced. There was a lot of mountain out there and only six experienced Mountaineers in their group. He tugged at Tony's arm, and they went into a huddle. Paula tried to catch what was being said, but they were deliberately keeping their voices down.

Tony reached into his pocket and pulled out a walkie-talkie. He handed it to Paula.

'You're our base. These things have a limited use up here, too many silent spots because of the way the rock is, but they are miles better than mobiles, as I'm sure you'll appreciate. If anyone gets back, let us know. You'll be able to listen in to what's going on. We'll leave Debbie with you, to keep you company.'

Paula had not noticed Debbie, who kept the post office, among the huddle of men. Debbie started to protest, not wanting to be pushed into the traditional waiting role. She wanted to be out on the mountain. Tony gave her a look, and she subsided into an angry mutter.

'I'd rather come out and look too,' Paula said, not wanting to wait helplessly, any more than Debbie did.

'You don't know the mountain,' Tony pointed out, as gently as he could, 'you'd be a liability. We need someone here, so we don't go on looking for someone who's made it back safely, all right?'

Paula nodded. She remembered her fantasies of walking on the mountain in Tony's company. She would never feel the same about that now.

Karen had turned back as the rain hit. The Old Woman had turned out to be just as harsh in reality as she had imagined. She hated the mountain with all the terror it instilled in her. It had nothing to recommend it. Her trainers slipped on wet rock and muddy earth, her jumper stretched as it got wet, so that the sleeves dripped and covered her hands, making it harder to keep a grip on anything she grabbed to keep her balance. Gorse reached out branches to scratch, heather roots twisted out of nowhere to trip her.

'I hate you,' she muttered under her breath, and the Old Woman threw a sudden blanket of fog at her.

'I fucking hate you,' Karen yelled at the top of her lungs, half laughing at her own stupidity in getting caught out by the Old Woman, after all her careful avoidance of her pitfalls, all her learning the tricks the mountain could try on her.

That's where losing you temper gets you, she thought, *out on a mountain with no map, in fog and rain*.

She stopped running, and turned a slow circle, trying to work out where she might be. There was nothing to be seen but the peaty earth, knee-high scrub and a blanket of cloud. Karen pushed hair out of her eyes, and tried to wipe the water off her face. A waste of time.

She could hear a distant sheep complaining. Not that that helped, the sheep roamed freely up here, and were no guide. She should never have left the track. The sheep paths here could lead you in circles, or dead ends, as well as any maze, even without a curtain of cloud to help the process.

Karen wished she had a whistle with her. That was what you were supposed to do, wasn't it? Take a whistle, and in trouble you blew it three times, or was that when you found someone in trouble, or were looking for…Anyway she hadn't got any damn whistle. She hadn't even got a coat.

George was sure he had heard a voice, distant, but definitely not a sheep. It was amazing how human sheep could sound. There was one peering down at him from the lip of the quarry, he could have sworn it had just spoken to him, surely it had said, 'Oh dear,' quite clearly.

'Help?' George suggested.

'Nah,' the sheep replied, and vanished from sight.

George tried once more to get upright, but he could not put any weight on his right arm in order to haul himself up, and he was reasonably sure he had a broken pelvis. He was surprised at how calmly he was taking this, lying there unable to move, no one to know where he was, except Karen.

'Help,' he tried again, louder – 'Help.'

He was sure he had seen Karen in the distance, that was how he had come to fall down here in the first place. He had been trying to attract her attention, not looking where he was going. Damn fool thing to do. He was getting horribly cold, lying here with the rain pouring into his eyes, into his nose, into his ears.

'Help,' he called again. Karen must come back this way, surely. She might be quite close, she would hear.

The trouble with silent spots on the mountain was becoming apparent. Paula listened helplessly to the hiss and crackle on the walkie-talkie. Debbie had shed her coat and jumper, and turned the heating back down, then sat opposite Paula at the table and wondered what on earth she was supposed to say. Tony would have had a better idea; he at least knew the family. The most she had had to do with any of the Randalls was to sell them a few stamps and pass the time of day.

The radio crackled into life.

'Found them,' a voice said, followed by a faint whistling, more crackling.

'Position?' Another voice, and the response a jumble of numbers, which meant nothing to Paula.

Debbie jotted the numbers down and consulted her map. She tapped the spot with her biro.

'Who do you have?' The same voice, perhaps Tony.

Crackling. Paula shook the radio.

'That won't help,' Debbie said, taking it from her.

'Base calling, repeat your last message, please,' she said, feeling important for the first time in this job.

'Parry. Both of them. Got that, Base?'

'Got it,' Debbie acknowledged.

Paula sighed, and took the radio back from Debbie.

Karen stumbled, and fell into a wall. A wall? She felt higher. Not a very high wall. She walked along it, hoping for a gate or stile. Yes, a gate. She climbed it stiffly, wiping the rust off her hands onto her jumper. She hated the smell of rust, it was like blood.

A road, of sorts, at least a farm track. She reviewed her memory of the map. Walled track, somewhere west and lower down the mountain than the lodge. That made it Ridge Farm, where they got the eggs...Karen stopped walking. She must be going the wrong way. She turned and looked up the track. Yes, there was a light. She started running.

The phone was ringing. Paula took the receiver with trembling hands.

'Paula? This is Kay, down at Ridge Farm. I've got your daughter here.'

'Which one?' Paula asked, hardly daring to think.

'Karen. She's very wet, so I've put her in the bath. I'll give her a lift back later okay? Have the boys found anyone else?'

'Yes,' Paula replied, feeling, for the first time, a part of this community.

Kay actually cared what happened to her, Kay's husband Graham was up the mountain this very moment looking for her errant family.

'Who?' Kay asked patiently.

'The Parry couple.'

'Well don't worry, Graham and the others are good at their job.'

Paula agreed that they were, and hung up. She let Debbie inform the rescue team of the latest development.

Davina followed her husband in a cold fury. They had been in real danger, and he had never for a moment doubted they would be rescued. He seemed incapable of giving credit to the rescue team for their very human efforts, and told them at some length that God was on his side. Davina felt this to be a slight to the men who had been forced to put themselves out, solely as a result of Howard's and her own stupidity.

Arriving back at the Lodge, the men stayed only briefly, to speak to Paula. Davina expressed her own gratitude somewhat gushingly, in an attempt to make up for Howard's failings. Michael was glad to have an excuse to leave, and hurried back up the mountain in search of the remaining idiots.

'Hell hath no fury like a mountain underestimated,' he observed to his companion, not for the first time. The Old Woman agreed; she hadn't enjoyed herself so much in ages.

Disturbed by the commotion, and the noisy plumbing, Anita woke from an exhausted sleep and crawled out from under Karen's bed, where she had gone to hide. Passing the Parry's door, she heard Davina shouting at her husband. The word divorce was mentioned more than once.

Oh good, Anita thought, as she stumbled on down the stairs, still half asleep. She wandered into the kitchen.

Paula looked up in astonishment. Anita stood in the doorway, barefoot, hair on end, her face swollen from George's fist: but completely dry, and clutching a large kitchen knife.

'Where have you been?' Paula asked, hugging her younger daughter to her, knife and all, and bursting into tears of angry relief.

'Careful,' Fiona hissed, as Ellen cannoned into her, 'there's a hell of a drop down there. Can you turn round, very carefully? I don't think we can get through.'

Ellen backed up a few steps, to where the path widened, and turned. Her legs were shaking with tension and cold. Fiona shuffled about until she could follow.

'Did you say something?' Ellen asked.

'No.'

'I thought I heard something: A voice?'

They stood for a moment listening. There was a voice calling, very faint.

'Do you think they've sent out the mountain rescue to find us?' Ellen asked hopefully.

'I hope not,' Fiona said, 'how humiliating.'

'Rubbish. You don't have the slightest idea where we are, do you? We need rescuing.'

'Go on then, call back.'

Ellen looked sheepish. She didn't actually want to admit to needing a rescue party when it came to it.

The voice reached them again.

'That's not a rescue party. They don't generally shout help.'

Fiona looked at Ellen, they weren't about to have to rescue someone themselves, surely?

'Where's it coming from?' she asked.

'Down there,' Ellen said, pointing over the edge of the quarry they had been skirting.

'What are we going to do?' Fiona asked.

Ellen edged onto her hands and knees and peered over the drop.

'Hello?' she called.

She couldn't actually see anyone, there was a gorse bush growing out of the side of the quarry just below her. She called again, and heard a faint response.

'Who are you?' she asked.

George could hardly believe it. Someone was there, asking who he was. He called back eagerly.

Ellen scrambled away from the edge.

'It's bloody George Randall,' she said.

Fiona looked surprised.

'What on earth is he doing out here?'

'Who cares?' Ellen asked, 'Come on, let's go.'

'We can't leave him.'

'Yes we can.'

'No,' Fiona said, 'We can't. One of us will have to go for help, and the other will have to stay here.'

'We don't know where to go for help,' Ellen shouted, 'I can't even read a map, so I can't go for help; and you needn't think I'm staying here on my own.'

'Then we'll have to get down there and do what we can for him, and wait for the mountain rescue to find us.'

'No. Absolutely not. We keep moving. There are only two quarries between where we were and the lodge if the map is to be believed. We have to be able to find the track from the bottom. We keep going, together. If we find a rescue party we send them back for him. I'm not putting myself out for that bastard.'

'Ellen, what the hell are you talking about?'

'He abuses his daughters.'

'That's not our business,' Fiona said, an automatic reaction, that she revised even as she spoke.

'No? Well neither is it our business to rescue the scum when he falls into a quarry. For all I know, one of his daughters pushed him in.'

Fiona grabbed Ellen's arm and shook her angrily. No matter what she thought of George Randall, there was an etiquette to being lost on mountains, of which Ellen was clearly unaware.

'Wake up, this is the real world. You can't just walk away from someone who's injured.'

'Yes I bloody well can. Watch me.'

Ellen grabbed the map from Fiona, and set off away from the lip of the quarry as fast as she could manage.

'Ellen!' Fiona called, infuriated, struggling after her.

Distantly, Ellen heard a sharp whistle. She turned back; to check that Fiona was following; then continued walking in as straight a line as the gorse would allow, in the direction of the whistle.

George shivered. He was so cold, and so weak, that he had started to hallucinate. He hoped Karen would find him soon. He blinked the water out of his eyes, peering up, expecting to see her making her way down the sheer side of the quarry. He could almost imagine her voice... *It's all right, dad, I'm here*...It was a long time since he had heard Karen say anything kind.

George had lost track of how long he had been lying there, with only the sheep for company. It really was amazing how human the sheep sounded, talking to each other in their comfortable, Home Counties accents. He could almost believe they were talking about him. The sheep didn't seem very sympathetic to his predicament on the whole, apart from one; he could have sworn he had heard a sheep ask him his name.

But it had wandered off as soon as he answered, as if thinking him not worth rescuing.

George could not think what he had ever done for the sheep to have so poor an opinion of him.

The Old Woman surveyed her domain.

Better, she thought; a little healthy respect for her more dangerous aspects should leave her undisturbed for quite a few months. And she should have done enough to close down that hotel. With the Randalls gone, she would have all the company she wished for-only the sheep and the occasional raven. Perfect.